## Daniel was different from any other man she'd ever known

He was kind. Patient. Funny. Appealing. Watching him play with the boys, she noticed the graceful way he moved, as if he were comfortable in his own skin.

Her gaze lingered, and a tingle ran through her. Well, of course, it was hard to be a female and not tingle at the sight of him. He was great to look at, but he wasn't just a pretty face. He radiated energy and life, and when he smiled, he could take her breath away.

There was danger here.

He must have sensed her looking at him, because suddenly he stopped, and then, slowly, sent her that smile of his. Lilah felt attraction dance down her spine like a caress, and without thinking, she found herself smiling back.

Dear Reader,

For most of us, family means everything. It's especially important to Daniel, Mike and Ian—the heroes of this three-book series—who grew up on their own, struggling to survive, until they met each other.

Becoming brothers by choice, they created the family they'd never had. By supporting and encouraging each other, the Foster brothers overcame their pasts and built new lives in Serenity Valley, an isolated community that has gradually accepted these newcomers.

This is Daniel's story. We hope you enjoy it and the two stories to follow, set in the beautiful Vermont countryside among people who cherish family above all. We love to hear from our readers. Feel free to drop us an e-mail at DalyThompson@aol.com.

Happy reading!

*Barbara and Liz*

# One of a Kind Dad

### DALY THOMPSON

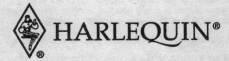

# HARLEQUIN®

TORONTO • NEW YORK • LONDON
AMSTERDAM • PARIS • SYDNEY • HAMBURG
STOCKHOLM • ATHENS • TOKYO • MILAN • MADRID
PRAGUE • WARSAW • BUDAPEST • AUCKLAND

Recycling programs
for this product may
not exist in your area.

ISBN-13: 978-0-373-75276-8

ONE OF A KIND DAD

Copyright © 2009 by Barbara Daly/Mary E. Lounsbury.

All rights reserved. Except for use in any review, the reproduction or
utilization of this work in whole or in part in any form by any electronic,
mechanical or other means, now known or hereafter invented, including
xerography, photocopying and recording, or in any information storage
or retrieval system, is forbidden without the written permission of the
publisher, Harlequin Enterprises Limited, 225 Duncan Mill Road,
Don Mills, Ontario M3B 3K9, Canada.

This is a work of fiction. Names, characters, places and incidents are
either the product of the author's imagination or are used fictitiously,
and any resemblance to actual persons, living or dead, business
establishments, events or locales is entirely coincidental.

This edition published by arrangement with Harlequin Books S.A.

® and TM are trademarks of the publisher. Trademarks indicated with
® are registered in the United States Patent and Trademark Office, the
Canadian Trade Marks Office and in other countries.

www.eHarlequin.com

**Printed in U.S.A.**

## ABOUT THE AUTHOR

Daly Thompson is a collaboration between Barbara Daly and Liz Jarrett, both multipublished authors. Barbara brings to this joint effort her passion for reading, the characters she's collected from the diverse places she's lived and jobs she's held, and a firm belief in happy endings. She began writing when she discovered she'd need a mobile career in order to follow her academic husband from coast (the Atlantic) to river (just across the Mississippi), and at last found her own happy ending in writing romance.

Liz has been writing stories since she was a child. After graduating from college, she was a technical writer for twelve years before she decided to stay home with her children. During their naps, she started writing her favorite type of stories—romances. This enjoyable pastime is now her full-time career.

Thanks to Johanna Raisanen for her expert guidance…and to my Vermont friends and neighbors. I wish I could have named a town after each of you.

# Chapter One

Nick's screams jolted Daniel into action before he was entirely awake. Barefooted, with his pajama bottoms flapping around his ankles, he raced down the hall, pausing outside Nick's room to take a deep breath and will his heartbeat to settle down. Not until he'd accomplished that did he step into the room.

"Nick," Daniel said softly. "It's okay. I'm here." He switched on the bedside lamp, a figure of a baseball player in a Red Sox uniform. In the subdued glow of the light, he saw the boy sitting up in bed, eyes wild and face drained of color, his screams still bouncing off the walls.

Daniel sat on the edge of the bed and smoothed Nick's tousled red hair. It was wet with perspiration. "It's okay," he said again. "I won't let anything hurt you."

Gradually, the screams faded into sobs, then to gasps for air. Nick didn't reach out his arms to be hugged until his terror passed. He'd been one of Daniel's foster boys for almost two months now, and still didn't trust him enough to seek him out for comfort. What could have happened to a boy so young to make him close his heart so completely?

No one knew. A woman in a larger town nearby had found Nick, all alone and unable to give his name or his parents' to Child Services. How old was he? The pediatrician who examined him had put his age at seven. Daniel's hands clenched. He'd solve the mystery of Nick one day, and when he did, the responsible parties would deeply regret what they'd done to this child.

"What's wrong?" Daniel asked, gently rubbing Nick's bony shoulder. "Tell me about it."

With one final gasp that ended on a sigh, Nick mumbled, "It was just a bad dream."

"What about?"

"Nothing."

"You'd feel better if you told me. We could talk about it."

"I don't remember. Sorry I woke you up."

Nick always said, "I don't remember." He was calm now, safe behind the invisible wall that protected him from the demons he couldn't confront.

"How about a little bedtime reading, then?" Daniel suggested. "What would you like to hear?"

*"The Swiss Family Robinson?"* It was not a statement so much as a question. *Is that okay with you—or am I asking too much?*

"Terrific," Daniel said. "My favorite."

In less than a minute he was back in Nick's room with the book, an old copy with yellowing pages. *The*

*Swiss Family Robinson,* in which the father was able to solve any problem that threatened his family's survival.

*If only.* The book offered a dream world in place of a nightmare world, and Nick clearly needed a glimpse of a dream world.

That's what Daniel had needed at Nick's age, as well. Routinely beaten by his father as his mother cried and wrung her hands, often before being knocked unconscious in her attempts to protect her son, Daniel had finally appeared in the local emergency room one time too many. Based on the testimony of medical staff and neighbors, he'd been taken from his parents and placed in a foster home.

But not a good foster home like the one he was giving Nick. In a series of miserable places, he'd slept on sofas, cut school to take care of younger children in his foster families, gone hungry, worn dirty clothes and been whipped for any infringement of a rule or shirking of a duty.

Daniel ran away from each of these homes, getting picked up, every time, only to be turned over to another family.

He lost his trust in human beings, thinking that no one would ever love him or even be kind to him. Still in his teens, he ran away again, and this time he was determined to run so far that no one could find him. He stole a bicycle and what little money his foster parents had around the house, grabbed a jar full of coins donated to charity from the general store counter and rode north as fast as he could. When he made the mistake of trying to cross over the border into Canada with a fanciful story but no ID, the border guards detained him for questioning. He could still feel the rage and frustration that made him fight back, injuring one of the guards before they could get him under control. Cuffed and helpless, he was sent back to Vermont and placed in juvenile detention. It was the best thing that could have happened to him, because there, at last, he'd found a family.

He and two other boys, Mike and Ian, discovered they had the same goal, to leave their unhappy pasts behind and become law-abiding and productive citizens. Slowly but surely, he'd learned to trust them. The three formed a strong bond, and when they were released from the facility they became "brothers," changing their surnames to Foster, and set out to change their lives.

Knowing he had people he could trust absolutely had been the turning point in Daniel's life. It had led him to taking in foster children—he had that one thing he could teach them, that in him they had someone they could trust, and that trust could eventually extend to other people, too.

So far, each of his foster kids had come to do that. And someday Nick would, too. But when? How could Daniel break through the boy's silence? Weekly visits to a psychiatrist hadn't worked any better than Daniel's own efforts.

Nick didn't want to be found by his real parents, and that told Daniel the whole story.

When the boy's eyes closed in spite of his attempts to stay awake, Daniel went back to his own room and fell into bed, emotionally drained, to struggle with his own nightmares.

"WE'RE GOING TO BE FINE, honey. I know it's scary to leave home for a new place, but I wouldn't bring you here if I didn't know it was the right thing to do, would I?" Lilah Jamison slid a sidelong glance at her son. Jonathan was scrunched down in the passenger seat, looking smaller and younger than usual, scared to death by this sudden upheaval.

Was it the right thing to do? She had $290, three-quarters of a tank of gas to get her from Whittaker, her hometown in the Northeast Kingdom of Vermont, to Serenity Valley, many miles south, a cooler packed with the contents of her refrigerator and not even an inkling of what she would do to support the two of them. But they'd be safe there. She'd researched every corner of Vermont before deciding that Serenity Valley was the perfect place to hide.

She had to hide, had to protect Jonathan and herself from her ex-husband, Jonathan's father. He'd been imprisoned for defrauding investors who'd trusted in him. Only a few people knew he'd also abused her. And now he was being released from prison. She'd been the one to blow the whistle on him, and she knew he was going to come after her as soon as he had the opportunity. Her muscles tightened, and her hands balled into fists on the steering wheel.

"Where will we live?" Those were the first words Jonathan had spoken in the past hour.

"We'll start by finding a special, secret place to park the car and set up housekeeping," Lilah said in a con-spiratorial whisper.

"Are we hiding out from the bad guys?" Jonathan turned toward her for the first time, looking interested.

She couldn't tell him the only "bad guy" in their lives was his father. She said, "Hmm. I was thinking we'd be more like *The Boxcar Children*." It was one of his favorite books. She hoped it would conjure up a positive image in his mind, even if it was less exciting than escaping from "the bad guys." "As soon as I get a job, we'll find a real house."

Or a one-room apartment like the one they'd lived in after she'd sold their three-bedroom cottage in Whittaker and used the money to pay off Bruce's remaining debts.

"What kind of work will you look for?"

"Well, I used to be a nurse," she reminded him. "Then, when you came along, I stayed home with you and did your father's bookkeeping." She could hardly bear to say the words. "And you know what I've been doing the past three years."

"Home care," Jonathan said. "For a nice, old lady."

"So I can look for several kinds of jobs. And you'll like your new school," she went on. "I just know it, because you make friends easily and you're a great soccer player."

"Yeah." He sighed. "Are we almost there?"

"The exit's coming up now. We'll take Route 30 for a few miles, and then we'll start looking for our hideout."

DANIEL WASN'T A CHURCHGOER himself, but he firmly believed in Sunday school for children. The boys griped and dragged their feet sometimes, but many of their best friends were kids they'd met at the Churchill Congregational Church, where they learned more about kindness than they did about any particular religion.

He'd finally herded the four of them, their hair still damp from showering and a few hands undoubtedly still sticky from pancake syrup, into the van. "Are we gonna have breakfast at the church?" Will asked.

"You just had breakfast," Daniel said, glancing into his rearview mirror to catch the eleven-year-old's eyes. "Seven pancakes, I think. A personal best."

"I know," Will said, "but sometimes they have real good stuff."

"I should hope so," Daniel said. "If you guys were ever ready in time to get there thirty minutes early, instead of eating breakfast at home in ten…"

"Yeah, yeah." Mutters came from the backseat. Daniel smiled. Kids who arrived thirty minutes before Sunday school began were served a hot breakfast. It had been his idea, and he still supported it financially. So much poverty existed in and around Churchill that he'd thought it would be a valuable service to the community. Besides, he owed the church something in return for suffering through an hour a week with his unruly gang. The program had been a big success.

As he pulled into the yard, he saw a small car, many years old, parked at the curb well away from the entrance to the building. It was dusty, as all Vermont cars were after negotiating the dirt farm roads into the town center, but otherwise it looked as if it had been well cared for.

A woman sat at the wheel, probably waiting for one of the children the breakfast program was intended to benefit. He could see little of her, just blond hair hiding her face as she bent over the steering wheel, reading, maybe, or just resting. His boys had already tumbled out of the van and gone on their way to rattle the cages of their long-suffering teachers.

Daniel thought about going to speak to her, offering to drive her child home after Sunday school so she wouldn't have to wait, but he decided against it. If she'd wanted company, she'd have gone into the church for the adult class.

Besides, he had a whole hour to himself, and what was he going to do with it? What any normal, virile, macho man would do. Go to the grocery store.

LILAH SAW THE CHILDREN begin to stream out of the church and looked anxiously for Jonathan. When she saw him, he was in deep discussion with a freckled redheaded boy about his age. Her muscles tightened. What she hated most about her situation was that she and Jonathan had to lie about themselves. But what if someday he forgot?

She got out of the car. She had to end the conversation before Jonathan became too chatty. When he saw her, he gave the other boy a wave and came running toward her, his eyes bright. She forced a big smile. She had to calm herself down—she couldn't start quizzing him about his conversation right away. "Did you have fun?" Lilah asked as they pulled away from the curb.

"Yeah." Jonathan looked happy.

"How was breakfast?" As she'd searched the grocery store bulletin board for job possibilities the day before, she'd seen a flyer inviting children to come for "breakfast and Bible study." Feeling desperately shy, she'd taken him into the church this morning, where he, to her relief, was greeted warmly.

"Great. We had pancakes and sausage and chocolate milk."

Lilah's stomach growled. "That does sound good," she said. She felt terrible about asking someone else to feed her child, but he hadn't had a hot meal in more than a week.

"And I made a friend."

"Now that is wonderful. What's his—or her—name?"

"His," Jonathan said, directing a brief "I hate girls" scowl at his mother. "Nick. He's nice."

"Tell me about him." *Please tell me you asked all the questions and didn't answer any.*

"He told me he's a foster child. What's a foster child?"

"Well, sometimes," Lilah said, dreading the inevitable consequences of giving Jonathan a definition, "parents can't take care of their own children. They have to let other people take care of them until they can get their lives in order."

"Is your life in order?"

"You and I are together and we always will be," Lilah said with a forced steadiness. "That's what I call having your life in order." How long could she keep up this pretense? A week of job-hunting had netted her nothing. But tomorrow could be different. *Would* be different. Because she'd never lose Jonathan to foster care, no matter how good that care might be.

"Who are Nick's foster parents?"

"He lives with a guy named Daniel. A vet... veternar..."

"Veterinarian," Lilah said.

"Vet-er-in-ar-ian. Some other boys live there, too, and a sort of grampa. His name is Jesse. Nick says they're all real nice."

"Really nice," Lilah said automatically.

"Yeah. But he looked real tired—*really* tired—and I asked him why, and he said he'd had another nightmare last night."

"Another nightmare?"

"He says he has 'em all the time."

"That's terrible," Lilah said, her heart going out to this child she didn't even know.

"Remember when I had those bad nightmares?"

How could she ever forget? Jonathan hadn't had one since he was three, when his father went to prison. Her child might be living in a car, eating cereal and sandwiches, but every night, when she'd tucked him into the backseat, he slept like Rip Van Winkle.

"I told him you made me a dreamcatcher, and I didn't have 'em anymore. I told him maybe you'd make one for him." He looked at her, the question in his eyes.

"Of course I will," Lilah said. "You could give it to him at Sunday school next week." She couldn't tell Jonathan the dreamcatcher had nothing to do with his nightmares going away. Even at three, he'd been far too aware of his father's brutality. He'd even tried to shield her from Bruce's fists with his small body. His father was his nightmare, and hers, but he'd left his nightmares behind with their source. Lilah still had a few. She hadn't found a job, and now she was down to $215.

"What color do you think he'd like?"

"Red and white. He likes the Boston Red Sox."

"Just like you." Lilah smiled. "Okay, red and white it is. Wow, that was quite a talk you had with Nick." Now, the quizzing. Lilah's hands tightened on the steering wheel. "Um, what did you tell Nick about yourself?"

"What you told me to. My father's dead and we moved here. And Mom, guess what the Sunday school lesson was about."

"What?" She was so relieved she could barely breathe.

"Telling the truth."

*God, forgive me.*

LOOKING OUT HIS WINDOW, Daniel saw the woman get out of the car and watched the boy run toward her. He might have called her pretty if she hadn't been so painfully thin and drawn. Her clothes were wrinkled, and her hair, although it was neatly combed, was dull and lank. But her posture was confident—determined was more like it—and it was clear that she and the boy loved each other. He was curious about her.

"Okay, spill it," he said to his passengers as they moved away from the curb. "How was Sunday school?"

Jason, almost sixteen and the oldest of his boys, spoke up first. "Not bad."

"The usual." Maury, a few weeks younger, was Jason's sidekick. "Another life lesson."

"Which *life lesson?*" Buzz words irritated Daniel, even when they came from the mouth of a Sunday-school teacher.

"Being honest."

"Us, too," Nick piped up.

"Ah," Daniel said. "A coordinated curriculum."

"Whatever," Nick said. "So this new kid asked me a question and I told him the truth."

A breakthrough! Had Nick told this boy the truth about where he came from?

*Act casual.* "What'd you tell him?"

"He said I looked tired, and I told him about my nightmares."

"What they were about?" The other boys had fallen silent, as if they were all holding their breath.

"I told you," he said. "I don't remember."

Hopes dashed, Daniel asked for and got a full report, not on the sin of lying but the inefficiency of it. And then they were home. Home to the scent of braising pot roast, to the comforting sight of Jesse carefully removing an apple crisp from the oven, to the racket of four boys shouting, arguing, laughing, racing up and down the stairs of the huge, creaky old Victorian house and the family dog, Aengus, barking, delighted they'd come back.

To Daniel, it sounded like the sweet strains of the Westminster Abbey boys' choir.

"LILAH JAMISON?"

"Yes." Lilah gave the portly manager of the Ben Franklin dime store a confident smile. *Don't be modest. Sell yourself. You have to, for your sake and Jonathan's.*

"I saw that you're looking for a person to handle your crafts section. I'm a crafter myself, and…"

"Already filled," the woman said. "Retha, she's one of our cashiers, says her daughter wants the job."

It wasn't the first time she'd gotten this response. Jobs in Churchill went to relatives of current employees. Lilah wanted to say, *But have you interviewed Retha's daughter? Does she know anything about knitting? Or decoupage? Or tole painting?* But it wouldn't matter. All that mattered was that she was Retha's daughter.

"Well," Lilah said, forcing another smile, "thanks for talking to me." She couldn't ask the woman to call her if she had another opening. She hadn't been able to afford a cell phone since Bruce had gone to prison. Her address, at the moment, was CWC 402, her license plate number. "While I'm here, I'd like to look at yarn."

Now that Lilah was a customer rather than a job applicant, the woman was all smiles. "You picked the right day," she said. "We're having a sale."

Lilah fought the tidal wave of discouragement threatening her belief that leaving Whittaker had been the right thing to do. First, she'd gone to the hospital to look for work as a hospital nurse or a home caregiver. "No openings in nursing," said the head of personnel, looking at her warily.

"I also have bookkeeping experience," Lilah said. "Would you have anything in Accounting?"

"No, but if something comes up, I'll give you a call."

But, of course, Lilah didn't have a phone number.

Since she'd arrived in Churchill, she'd followed up
on every job offer on the grocery store bulletin board
and in the classified ads of the local newspaper. There
weren't many. Apparently Churchill folks didn't hire
cleaning ladies. And the school didn't need cafeteria
workers or teachers' aides.

She dropped in at the local diner. "My husband's
the short-order cook, my daughter and I are the wait-
resses, and we hire the intellectually challenged to bus
tables and clean up," the woman at the counter told
her. "Sorry."

Before she picked up Jonathan at the park, where
she'd discovered the town ran an informal, drop in,
drop out, day care in the summer months, Lilah took
one last look at the grocery store bulletin board. No job
offers, but a brightly colored poster caught her eye:

### *Fair Meadows Soccer Camp*
*Attention, future soccer stars aged five to sixteen!*
*Coach Wetherby and the Town of Churchill offer*
*you this opportunity to sharpen your skills for*
*competitive team play!*
*Nine to noon, Monday through Friday*
*at Friendship Fields.*
*All Serenity Valley students welcomed.*
*Sign up now!*
*Registration fee includes...*

Lilah's eye stopped at "registration fee." Jonathan
excelled at soccer. He could make friends at the camp,
and then he wouldn't have to enter second grade as the

"new kid." The fee wasn't much, but she couldn't afford a fee of any size.

It was the last straw. "Go team," she whispered. They'd have to go without Jonathan. His mother had missed one goal too many.

She hurried out of the store before she fell apart. What was she going to do? Would she have to move to a larger town outside the valley, where she'd find more job opportunities?

"I have an idea," she told Jonathan when she picked him up, giving him a smile that took all the optimism she could muster. "Let's blow it all out at the diner—hamburgers, French fries, the works—and then we'll drive back to our secret hideout and make Nick a dreamcatcher."

## Chapter Two

Daniel eyed the mountain of laundry on the basement floor, started a load, stalked up the steep stairs and said, "Jesse, we need a housekeeper."

"Last thing we need's a woman around here," Jesse said. "They don't have their priorities straight. Want things to look pretty before they really do anything."

A typical reaction from Jesse O'Reilly. A long-retired marine and a widower for many years, he'd been renting the apartment over the carriage house when Daniel bought the property. Because any income to offset Daniel's investment was a plus, he'd encouraged Jesse to stay.

Then, when Daniel took in his first foster child, Jason, a rebellious, fighting-mad fourteen-year-old at the time, Jesse had told Daniel if he ran into a problem, he should just call and he'd keep an eye on the boy. And slowly, Daniel had begun to trust Jesse. He took in more boys, and Jesse became even closer to the family, somehow having dinner ready before Daniel got back from picking up the kids after school, somehow producing stacks of laundered clothes, a full cookie jar.

Last year Jesse had fallen down the apartment stairs, and Daniel had talked him into moving into the house. Now he was chef, chauffeur, child-sitter, homework supervisor—and Daniel's best friend, next to his brothers. More like a father than a friend. A grumpy father with a heart of pure homemade spaghetti sauce.

"Let me put it another way," Daniel said. "You work sixteen hours a day, the boys have their chores, we all help clean on Saturday, but if you could see the condition upstairs you'd have us court-martialed." He was exaggerating, but not by much.

Jesse, who was even now engrossed in dinner preparations while the boys—Jason and Maury, Will and Nick—did their homework at the kitchen table, spun around from his stovetop. "It's dirty?" he gasped.

"Criminally," Daniel assured him. "If Child Services came around, they'd take the kids away." Thinking that might scare the younger boys, he gave them a wink, and they gave him a thumbs-up. "Then there's the laundry. Imagine Mount Everest."

"You're the one won't let me go down those stairs any more," Jesse grumbled.

"For good reason," Daniel said. "The housekeeper doesn't have to be a woman, but whoever it is, I won't let him or her get in your way."

"Well, okay, look around." His nose in the air, Jesse turned back to the stove. "Just don't let anybody mess with my kitchen."

"Why would I do that?" Daniel asked. "It's the cleanest room in the house."

"THIS IS A FUNNY WAY to wash clothes," Jonathan said.

"But it works," Lilah told him, smiling brightly and trying to hide the sickness she felt inside. "The sun dries them, they smell fresh and sweet… This is the way the pioneers did their laundry. How about a bologna-and-cheese sandwich before I take you to the park?"

Their hideout hadn't been easy to find. After scouring the back roads of the three towns that made up the valley, Lilah had found, just outside Churchill, a lumber road that led up to a forested area, beautiful and serene, with no heavy equipment around to indicate that the trees were marked to be cut any time soon. This is where she and Jonathan were living. They slept in the car, bathed in the icy stream and washed their clothes there, leaving them to dry in the dappled sunlight.

They ate cereal and milk, sandwiches made of the least expensive sandwich meat and cheese, or peanut butter and jelly, with a piece of fruit for Jonathan each day. Lilah ate as little as she could without making herself feel faint, saving everything possible for her son. They'd been living like this for almost two weeks now. She couldn't hold out much longer. It wasn't fair to Jonathan.

"What do you think about the dreamcatcher?"

"It's great," Jonathan said, his face lighting up.

Together they admired her handiwork. She'd cut a circle out of a cereal box and had painted it with scarlet nail polish she'd found among the things she'd hastily thrown into garbage bags when they left Whittaker. When had she ever worn bright-red nail polish? Long years ago, when she was still in love with Bruce and had no idea what he would eventually do to her, to their lives? The love hadn't lasted long. The bottle of polish had been almost full.

When the polish dried, Lilah filled in the circle with the yarn she'd bought, a twisted red and white, and then she attached red-painted twig arms and legs, crocheting fanciful feet and hands to fit over the twigs.

In a moment of whimsy, she crocheted a baseball cap and attached it to the top of the circle. A Boston Red Sox dreamcatcher. And then, giving it one last critical look, she decided it needed a catcher's mitt.

"Is Nick right- or left-handed?" she asked Jonathan.

Jonathan looked at her as if she'd asked a pretty dumb question, but then he thought about it. "Left," he said suddenly, "because when there's a new kid at Sunday school everybody writes himself a name tag, and Nick was sitting over here," he gestured to his right, "so our elbows kept bumping and we thought it was funny and that's when we started talking."

"You're a great detective," Lilah congratulated him. So she'd crocheted the mitt onto the left toothpick hand, smiling to herself as she worked.

Making the dreamcatcher had been as good for her as she hoped it would be for Nick. It was the first time in ages she'd found anything humorous to think about her in life.

"Okay, kiddo," she said, giving him that forced bright smile. "Off to the park."

And back to her desperate job search. This week, she didn't even have to buy the *Valley News*. Someone had left a copy on a park bench, which she spotted after dropping Jonathan off at the soccer field. In the classified ads section, she read, "Single father is seeking housekeeper. Call 802.555.4432. References essential."

It was as if an angel had left the newspaper for her to find. She felt a glimmer of excitement, and then the glimmer began to shine. It would be a perfect job for her.

She had no references, however. If she asked for one from the son of the woman she'd cared for these past three years she'd be letting him know where she was, and she didn't want anyone in Whittaker to know where she was. She raised her chin resolutely. She'd have to convince this single father that she'd be the housekeeper of his dreams, references or not.

Gathering change from the bottom of her handbag, knowing every penny had to be spent carefully, she sought out the pay phone on Main Street and dialed the number. If no one answered, she'd just have to call again and again. In her mind's eye she saw dollars and dollars clinking through that slot...

"'Lo."

She blinked. She hadn't expected such a gruff, grumpy voice. "I'm calling to apply for the housekeeping job," she said. The assured voice she'd planned on using came out timid and shaky.

"He's working now," the voice said, skipping several conversational steps. "What's your number? He'll call you back tonight."

This time, Lilah got her voice to cooperate. "I don't have phone service just now," she said. "Is there a time I could drop by?" She held her breath and crossed her fingers.

Silence. Then, "Ay-uh. Might talk to you around five. In his office." He gave her the address. "Side door," he added.

Limp with relief, Lilah almost slid to the sidewalk. She had an interview. At five o'clock this afternoon she *would* get that job. She had to.

"ANOTHER APPLICANT," Jesse told Daniel.

Daniel blew a breath into the hands-free mouthpiece of his cell phone. "When can I talk to her?"

"She made an appointment. I told her five—figured that would work."

Daniel sighed. "I didn't realize how much time it would take just to hire a housekeeper. What's your take on that first one I talked to last night?"

"She gossips. Everybody knows it."

"Hmm. The next one had an excellent reference."

"From Shaw's Supermarket, yes. If you were needing a butcher, then she'd be your woman."

Daniel had disliked the other two he'd met after five minutes with each of them. "You're not much help," he grumbled.

"I'm not too excited about this housekeeper idea."

"Duh," Daniel said, and frowned. "Well, okay, I'll make the decision about the one who's coming in this afternoon. I'm not even going to let you see her."

"Humph," Jesse said, and hung up.

It was a busy afternoon. Jesse had caught Daniel on the way to the Dupras farm to check on Maggie, a prize-winning pig who should be delivering her piglets in the next few days. After he'd seen Maggie, he went back to the office to see two cats, a dog, a mynah bird who called him "pond scum" in a radio announcer's voice and a boa constrictor that kept wrapping itself around Daniel's arm.

He was still a little rattled by the snake's fondness for him when Mildred, his receptionist—actually, she did everything except practice medicine—put her head through his office door and said, "Your five o'clock is here. No pet." She gave Daniel a quizzical look.

"Housekeeper applicant," he said.

"Hmm," she murmured. "Can you see her now?"

"Sure. Whoever she is, she can't be worse than the snake."

Mildred shuddered and went back to the waiting room.

A minute later, he heard a timid knock on the door. The woman who stepped in wasn't what he expected, not at all like the other applicants. She couldn't be more than thirty, but her face looked old with worry. She was tall, or at least not short. Her sedate dress was clean but wrinkled, and her blond hair hung limply around her shoulders...

Hadn't he said the same thing to himself about some other woman recently? Yes, she was the woman he'd seen at the church, the one whose little boy had made friends with Nick.

She hadn't seen him there, he thought, so he wouldn't mention it. He stood and held out his hand. "Daniel Foster," he said.

"Yes," she said, shaking his hand, "Lilah Jamison."

Her hand was damp, and she was trembling. "Good of you to come by," Daniel said. "Have a seat. So you're new in town?"

"Yes." Her voice grew firmer. "My husband died, and my son and I needed a fresh start."

He nodded. "You have references?"

She flushed, but she looked him straight in the eye. "I'm afraid not. I've never worked as a housekeeper but I've always kept a spotless house, even though I worked full-time." She stared him down as if she expected him to say, *Sure you did.*

"What sort of work did you do?"

When she told him she'd been a nurse doing home care, it occurred to him that it wouldn't be bad having a nurse in the house to deal with four risk-taking boys. But his attention was distracted by how desperate she looked.

She wasn't merely thin, but haggard. The half-moons under her eyes, which were dark blue, indicated sleep deprivation and worry; lusterless hair suggested a poor diet. A modest sundress showed off arms that were too thin. Ivory skin that might once have been beautiful was now dry and lifeless. Her husband's death must have thrown her a knockout punch. Either he had been much older than she, or he'd died tragically young.

And she had a little boy. His blood suddenly ran cold. How could she take care of a child in her condition?

This was hitting him too close to home. The boy— what kind of life was he living? Nick had liked him. Nick was scared of his own shadow, so her son couldn't be a bully or a troublemaker. But still, Daniel was looking for a housekeeper for *his* kids and he was taking no chances.

"Why didn't you take a nursing job?" he asked, keeping his voice gentle. "The Churchill hospital is—"

"Filled with nurses already." He saw her face tighten, but she didn't sound bitter.

"I understand," he said, and he did. "Nepotism" wasn't in the local vocabulary. It was simply understood that jobs were passed down from generation to generation. "You seem like a pleasant person, which is important to me, since you'd be keeping house for four foster children. But without references—"

She seemed to sag in her chair.

"Tell you what," he said, starting to think that perhaps because this woman needed help so badly he could trust her to do the job well. "Give me your address and phone number and I'll call you with my final decision. I've had several applicants," *dreadful ones,* he reminded himself, "and I need to think things over."

"As you said, we're new here. No phone service yet." He could tell she was trying to be matter-of-fact, but he could also see the pain in her eyes. "I'll come by the clinic in a few days. You could leave a message with your assistant."

She stood up, too, and just as Daniel held out his hand to shake hers again, he heard a familiar sound, one of the boys coming to tell him about some wonderful— or terrible—thing that had just happened.

"Daniel!"

"Mom!"

His job applicant rushed toward the boy who'd yelled, "Mom," and said, "Honey, you were supposed to stay outside…"

But Nick drowned her out. "This is Jonathan, the one I was telling you about. I saw him in his car, and he said he had a present for me. Look what his mom made!"

Daniel, not as rattled as he had been about the snake but close to it, moved around his desk to stare at the weird thing Nick held in his hand. It could be a voodoo doll. No voodoo in his house. Or it might be a Satanic totem.

A Satanic totem that looked like a Red Sox baseball player?

He tried to clear his head. "That was kind of you," he said to the mysterious Lilah Jamison, who had an arm around her son. "What is it?"

"A dreamcatcher," she answered for Nick. Then she relaxed her hold on Jonathan and turned her attention to Nick, her voice soft and musical. "It captures bad dreams before you dream them. You told Jonathan you have nightmares, but if you really and truly believe in it, we're sure this dreamcatcher will bring an end to them."

"I do believe in it," Nick said reverently. "Jonathan told me it worked for him. Look at it, Daniel," Nick said. "It even has a catcher's mitt on its left hand!"

Daniel admired this thing they called a dreamcatcher, then gazed at Lilah's son. He was a little taller than Nick, with his mother's blond hair and deep-blue eyes. But he didn't have his mother's look of despair. Whatever had befallen them, Jonathan was a happy child.

His gaze moved toward Lilah, and she must have had that feeling of being watched, because she looked up at him at once. "I think you've just provided your reference," he said, ruffling Jonathan's hair, "and he's an excellent one."

Her eyes widened. "Thank you," she said.

He'd decided he could trust her to be good with the boys. Even if she wasn't a perfect housekeeper, any assistance would be an improvement. He needed help, she needed help—they could help each other and everybody would be better off.

"I'd like the rest of the family to meet you before I make a final decision, and you should meet them so you know what you'd be getting into," he said. "Stay for dinner. It's the best way to catch them all at once."

He saw Jonathan's gaze turn on her, but she gave him a quick glance and said, "Oh, I'm not sure we should…"

"It's some kind of chicken stew, it smells great, and there's apple pie for dessert."

"Mom?" The look in Jonathan's eyes was a dead giveaway.

"Well, I…" She was wavering.

Then she turned to Daniel. Her determined expression made him sure she'd say no, but she surprised him. "Thank you for your invitation," she said formally. "We accept."

Nick and Jonathan sped away, cheering. Lilah looked limp. "Thank you for seeing me," she said. "I know you're busy, so I'll just wait outside."

"Look around, if you want to," Daniel said. "I'm warning you. It's a big place." He opened the back door of the clinic, which led into the house.

She gave him a slight smile. "I'm not afraid of hard work."

*You're afraid of something,* Daniel thought as she ignored the open door and went instead through the waiting room into the yard. He shook his head. She was running scared, and he wished he could figure out why.

IN THE YARD, LILAH tried to still the trembling of her hands. She wanted and needed this job so badly. But she hadn't intended to become a member of Daniel Foster's family. She'd imagined herself slipping in at nine and out at five, a human vacuum cleaner, nothing more. This situation might be too intimate. She'd wanted to stay invisible. But she had to have a job. For Jonathan's sake. And this one was her best bet.

Worry was wearing her out. To distract herself, she studied the house. The patterned wood shingles were painted lavender, with the molding details picked out in dark purple and turquoise. It was an enormous place, with a turret rising into the sky. She'd entered the clinic through a separate entrance that had its own stoop and overhang, with a discreet brass plaque on the door that read, Serenity Valley Veterinary Clinic, Daniel Foster, DVM. and in front of it, the small graveled parking area where she'd left her car.

She gazed back at the fancifully painted building. The man she'd just met didn't look like a lavender, purple and turquoise kind of person. She'd read his name on the door plate, wondered if he could be the Daniel who was Nick's foster father, and was expecting to see an old, fatherly country vet, not someone close to her own age, undeniably masculine, tall, lean and muscular. She'd felt a moment of fright when she walked into his office, and she wondered—would the sight of a large, powerful man always have this effect on her?

The thought was enough to dim her mood, her hopes, the illusion of confidence she'd been able to maintain after that first uncomfortable minute. If Daniel offered her the job, she'd stay as far away from him as she could.

He *seemed* to be a kind person. His sandy hair, which fell across his forehead, made him look boyish. His eyes were an interesting color—mocha, she'd call it. They were thoughtful eyes, assessing, analyzing her while they talked.

But you never knew. Bruce had been attractive, too. And she'd let herself become dependent on him; too dependent to run away from his abuse, too afraid she couldn't raise Jonathan on her own.

His years in prison had changed her. Now, even though she had no money, she was independent. Confident in her ability to give Jonathan the important things—love, support, emotional security. She'd never again let a man take control of her life. But just being a housekeeper wouldn't be taking a risk, would it?

Daniel appeared at the back door. "Come on in," he said. "Dinner's almost ready."

*Here we go. My future and Jonathan's depend on the next few hours.*


DANIEL HADN'T CALLED THE boys to dinner yet. He wanted them to barrel in one or two at a time, as they usually did, so Lilah wouldn't grab her son and run screaming from the chaos.

The fact that the kitchen was relatively empty seemed to unnerve her for a second, but then he saw her face as she took in her surroundings. The old-fashioned maple cupboards, which rose high enough so that even he needed a stepladder to reach the upper ones, the big range and the even bigger refrigerator. The old brick floor, worn smooth by the feet of several generations of occupants. The round table that sat in the middle of the room surrounded by mismatched chairs. The table centerpiece: a bicycle helmet instead of flowers.

He couldn't read her expression. Was she thinking it wasn't quite as clean as a kitchen should be for a houseful of children? Was she appalled by the oilcloth cover on the table? If that was it, was she out of her mind? Did she have any idea what laundry problems real tablecloths and napkins would cause?

He reminded himself to postpone showing her the laundry piled in the basement until after she'd accepted the job.

"Jesse, meet our job applicant, Lilah Jamison. She and her son are staying for dinner."

Jesse, stirring something in a gigantic pot, wheeled around on his good leg. "Major Jesse O'Reilly at your service, ma'am." Having done his duty, he whirled back to the stove. Jesse didn't want a housekeeper, and he'd spoken pretty crisply. Then he stopped stirring, and slowly turned back to take another look at Lilah. His expression changed. Daniel could tell that now he was seeing her not as a potential interloper, but simply as a nice-looking young woman who needed feeding.

Jesse dipped a spoon into the pot and held it aloft.

"Mind tasting this stuff?" he asked her. "Might need more salt."

She joined him at the stove, instantly looking comfortable with the situation she'd walked into. "It's just right," she told him, licking her lips.

"When's dinner?" Nick and Jonathan shot through the door, Nick yelling the question at Jesse.

"Hold on, hold on," Jesse grumbled, and focused his attention on Jonathan.

"This is Jesse," Nick said to Jonathan.

"And this is Jonathan, Lilah's son," Daniel explained.

Jesse gave Jonathan the same thoughtful gaze he'd given Lilah. "I need a junior opinion on this stew," he said, and handed spoons to the boys.

Daniel wondered if Jesse was starting to look a little obvious. At just the right time, Will raced in through the door. "Brunswick stew," he shouted. "I could smell it all the way upstairs."

"Hey, Will, you almost knocked Nick over."

Daniel smiled at Jason, noticing how his voice had deepened even more in the past few weeks, seeing how he ruffled Will's hair and smiled even as he scolded him.

"You said four boys?" Lilah murmured, looking stunned by the sudden frenzy of activity.

"Yeah, it just feels like more. That's why we do a lot of yelling around here. Have to, if you want anybody to hear you. Meet Jason, he's the blond one—and Maury, the one who looks like a football player, which he is. This is Lilah, and this is Jonathan. Did anybody let Aengus in?"

"I'll do it," Jason said.

"We're moving in on it, kids," Jesse said. "Grab a couple of those round loaves of bread out of the pantry, Sergeant Jamison. Step lively. It's that door over there." He pointed with his stirring spoon and juices dripped on the floor.

"The rest of you boys get that table set and everybody sit down. You're startin' to make me dizzy."

NOBODY'S LIFE COULD BE this good. The boys threw cutlery and plates haphazardly onto the table and sat down at once, including Jonathan. Shyly, Lilah joined them.

"What can I get you to drink? Water? Wine? Beer from my secret stash?"

"Water, please," she said, "and thank you." Secret stash? He was a closet drinker? While he harbored a houseful of foster boys, he drank himself into oblivion night after night?

"Good choice," he said. "I was down to my last beer—I have one every Saturday night after I get the kids to bed, and the wine is the stuff Jesse uses for his fancy beef stews. The alcohol boils off," he explained, as if he thought she might be planning to report him for serving wine to children.

So. Not a big drinker. He had to have a different fatal flaw. All men had a fatal flaw.

Or maybe just the ones who'd had some impact on her life.

Already stretched as tight as a bungee cord, every bone in her body went stiff when the biggest dog she'd ever seen leapt into the room and ran directly toward Jonathan. She gasped, jumping up so rapidly she knocked over her chair.

Before she could rescue her son, if it was possible to rescue him from a beast this huge, the dog had set to work licking Jonathan's face. Jonathan was giggling uncontrollably, hugging the animal.

She picked up her chair and sat down. "I see he's friendly," she said, feeling limp as a frozen celery stalk. "What—is he?"

"An Irish wolfhound," Daniel said, "who's way too big to be way too friendly." In a quiet tone, he said, "Aengus. Sit."

Aengus sat.

"Stay," Daniel said.

Aengus stayed.

Jason came back and Jesse called out over the cacophony of voices, "Chow's on!" He put a huge serving of stew in front of Lilah and another in front of Jonathan, then began serving the rest of them, including a plate for the dog, who didn't move until Daniel said, "Okay." A basket of hot bread and a stick of butter in a plastic refrigerator container followed, then a huge plastic bowl of salad. The noise level was deafening as the boys ate and talked at the same time.

The stew was delicious, a rich combination of chicken and vegetables. Lilah tried to eat slowly, signaling to Jonathan not to gobble his food. But all the kids were eating as if they hadn't eaten in months.

"Everything okay?" Daniel said.

She turned to look at him. "It's excellent. Thank

you," she said, hearing the faintness of her voice. She felt overwhelmed by...

By what, she wasn't sure. When she turned back to her plate, she saw that Jesse had refilled it. Out of the corner of her eye she saw him putting not one but three pies into the oven to warm.

What overwhelmed her was the realization that this was a happier family than either she or Jonathan had ever known. Her parents had been poor and they'd resented it, never showing her the love they must have felt for her, their only child. They'd never shared a meal like this one, gathered around a table and laughing together. As for Jonathan's life with her and Bruce... Lilah's throat tightened, and she rose from the table.

"This has been wonderful, but we should go now," she managed to say before Daniel leapt up just as rapidly.

He took her arm and turned her away from the boys, saying, "I'd like to talk to you for a few minutes. You guys get on with it. Save us some pie." He closed the door on the chaotic scene and began to hurry her down the hall.

"No!" she said, tugging her arm away from him. "I'm fine. Let me go back to the kitchen."

Taken aback, Daniel halted and turned to look at her. She glared back at him. "Why?" was all he could think of to say.

"I don't want to leave Jonathan alone."

"Alone with four other boys and a retired marine?"

"Alone without me. And I don't want to be alone with you."

He spoke as soothingly as he could. "Look, something upset you in the kitchen, and I thought you might like some privacy."

"I would," she said. Her voice was strained. "I really appreciate your hospitality, but now I want to take my son home."

"As soon as we talk." Lilah was chewing off her own foot, taking herself and her child away from something they'd both obviously enjoyed.

"All right. We'll talk." Stiffly, she followed him into the living room. And that was the right word for it—signs of living were everywhere, with books, games, bats and balls, this and that dropped here and there.

"Have a seat. How about some coffee? Relax a minute and I'll bring you some." Daniel knew she wouldn't leave without her son, but he hurried out anyway, leaving her sitting straight as a fencepost on the cracked leather sofa. When he came back she was still sitting there, looking slightly less combative.

He handed her one of the coffee mugs, stretching out his arm as far as it would go and not coming any closer to her than he had to, as if she were a feral cat. Then he sat down in the chair that was farthest from her chosen corner.

"I suppose this means I've lost my chance to get the job," she said as if she'd rehearsed the lines in his absence. "I did get a little...upset. I guess I'm tired and overemotional."

He nodded. "Moving is stressful. But, no, you haven't lost your chance. In fact, you seem to be exactly the housekeeper we've been looking for."

It was painful for Daniel to see the relief that

flooded her face. "So give me your address, and I'll drop you a note."

"As I said earlier, I'll come to the clinic in a few days to find out what you decided."

Daniel's chest tightened. "You don't have a phone, you don't have an address—you're homeless, aren't you?"

She flushed with embarrassment. "That's none of your business."

"Lilah," he said, "look around you. Making sure kids are being taken care of *is* my business."

"I'm taking very good care of Jonathan," she said. Her voice shook and her eyes glittered with tears. "He's the most important thing in my…"

"Mom!" Jonathan ran into the room, so excited he looked as if he might pop. "Can I spend the night with Nick? He thinks I'd help the dreamcatcher work better."

Aengus bounded in right behind Jonathan, and Nick followed with a precariously loaded tray holding wedges of apple pie. He pushed aside the things that already littered the coffee table and set down the tray. "Please?" Jonathan said. His eyes were shining.

Daniel desperately wanted Lilah to say yes—for Nick, who looked so happy, and for Jonathan, her homeless son. "That sounds like a great idea to me," he said, raising a hand to warn Aengus against stealing the pie.

"Jonathan, we've imposed ourselves on these people long enough. It's time to go home. So say goodbye and thank you and we'll—"

"But Mom, we don't—"

Lilah stiffened, and Jonathan grew quiet.

"Tell you what," Daniel said easily, "your mom and I will discuss it. You guys can find something to do for five minutes, right?" He'd had a brilliant idea.

When the boys had left, he faced Lilah, whose face was pale and rigid. "You do understand that what I need is a live-in housekeeper," he said.

Her expression changed. "Sure," she said bitterly. "I knew there was a catch. No, thank you. I don't need a job that badly."

"Not living in this house," he said. Exasperation rose in him, too, in response to her implication. "There's an apartment over the carriage house—Jesse used to live there. You can stay there tonight and check it out."

"I'd be very glad to take the housekeeping job," she said. Her lips were drawn and white. "But not a live-in job."

"I'm afraid," he added, even more determined now, "that I'll have to insist on the housekeeper living on the premises. With all these kids, she can't help but be a housemother, too."

"Thank you, but I'm going home, and tomorrow I'll look for a job that won't require us to live in." She started toward the door.

"Think about Jonathan. Do it for him."

She spun toward him and pushed back her hair. "I think about nothing but Jonathan," she said. "And I think about how I'm never going to let him fall under the spell of a man who's all nice and charming at first and then…"

When she pushed back her hair, Daniel saw the scar on her forehead—a jagged scar than ran from her temple to just above her eyebrow. It wasn't a fresh wound, but it was too recently healed to have been the result of a childhood accident. A car wreck, maybe, or a serious fall on the ice, but somehow he didn't think so. A blow from her deceased husband? A recent boyfriend? Daniel's protective instincts boiled up inside him. Where had her son been when this happened to her?

"Then what?" he asked, saying it as casually as a shop clerk might say, "Anything else?" And all the while, his gut clenched and twisted, just as if the young, suspicious Daniel was struggling to get loose.

Her lips tightened. "Nothing. Goodbye."

"The carriage house door has a lock. The apartment door has a lock. You'll be safe, and Jonathan will be right next door. A night in a good bed, a hot shower, one of Jesse's breakfasts, and you'll be in much better shape for job-hunting."

She hesitated, turned back, searched his face, and thank God, she must have seen only the calm adult Daniel. Or she'd thought about the good bed, the hot shower, a big breakfast. But he had a feeling she was seeing it for Jonathan, not for herself.

She loved her son, and he loved her. She could have faked it, but a child couldn't. That, to Daniel, was the key to what she was as a person—a caring human being, a woman who'd somehow lost control of her life.

All at once she seemed to deflate. The embarrassment and anger were gone, and resignation took their place. "One night," she said. "And Jonathan may spend the night with Nick."

Daniel's face still felt tight. "Fine," he said. "Jesse has the carriage house keys. You can give Jonathan the good news. I'll stay out of your way." He stalked toward the door, then turned back to face her. "The job is yours if you want it." He glanced at the coffee table. "Don't forget your pie."

It was a relief to turn his back on her startled face. When he got to his room, he sank onto the bed. It hadn't been a pretty scene, but he'd gotten the result he wanted. Lilah would spend the night in the carriage house instead of her car, and Jonathan would be safe and warm and surrounded by boys who were delighted to have him there, especially Nick, who needed one more little leap of faith to help the dreamcatcher do its work.

Lilah's scar lingered in Daniel's thoughts, entered into his dreams and then kept him awake until the midnight call that meant he had to throw on clothes, alert Jesse that it was his watch and speed to the Dupras farm, where Maggie, the prize sow, had gone into labor.

A woman in distress always got him up and running, even when she was a pig.

WITH A FEELING THAT she was falling into a trap, Lilah made her way through the darkness to her car to retrieve the big trash bag into which she'd thrown her clothes before leaving Whittaker. She took note of the silver van and bright red pickup parked where a carriage would once have sat, then slowly climbed the stairs to the living quarters.

She unlocked the door, stepping inside to find a self-contained apartment, clearly a man's world, but neat and clean. No coachman had ever lived in such splendor. Lilah set down her modest bag of possessions and put the wedge of pie next to the bed. She was stunned by all that had happened in just a few hours. She'd broken her own promise to herself and had put her life and Jonathan's into someone else's hands, even if it was only for a night. What had she been thinking?

Slowly she went toward the door that had to lead to the bathroom, opened it and looked inside. For the first time in two weeks, she could take a shower!

Giddy with excitement, she dug out her toiletries and arranged them on the granite counter, stripped off her clothes and turned on the water. She stepped under the steaming spray and let out a deep sigh of pleasure.

The water streamed through her hair, over her shoulders, down her back. She reveled in it, washing away all her worries, if only for a few minutes. She poured shampoo into her hand and lathered it into her hair. It smelled faintly of flowers. Flowers in the rain. She wanted to stay in the shower until everything was all right again.

The bathroom was warm when she stepped out, wrapped herself in a towel and looked in the mirror. She looked different, she felt different. Something buzzed through her body, making her feel alive again. With a start, she realized that what she was feeling was hope.

# Chapter Three

Lilah woke early, more rested than she'd felt in years. She took another shower and spent a few minutes styling her hair as well as she could without a hair dryer— she'd forgotten hers, and why would an ex-marine with a buzz cut have a hair dryer? A swish of mascara, a bit of powder on her nose, lip gloss.

She didn't want Daniel's charity. He'd given her and her son shelter for the night. She had to pay him back, and she'd figured out how she might do it.

She dug into her bag of clothes and searched for something relatively clean and not as wrinkled as the sundress she'd taken off the night before. Tan trousers and a pale-blue shirt were the best she could do. Leaving the apartment in perfect order, she set off toward the main house.

Daniel's big silver van was still in its spot, but the little red pickup was gone. She stepped through the dewy grass toward the house where Jonathan slept now, happier than he'd been in weeks.

Shivering in the chill of a June morning in Vermont, Lilah approached the kitchen door to find it locked.

Inside, she could hear Aengus barking. In trying to surprise them, she'd probably awakened the whole household.

She spent a minute biting her lower lip, then circled the building, wondering which room was Nick's. When she saw a Red Sox pennant taped to a window, she smiled. That was a clue.

She tapped on the window and called Jonathan's name, softly at first, then a little louder. Apparently even Aengus couldn't wake up these boys.

A tousled blond head appeared at last, and Jonathan raised the window. "Mom?"

"Good morning," she said, smiling at him. "Unlock the kitchen door for me, okay? I want to surprise everybody and cook breakfast."

A second tousled head appeared. "Can we help?" Nick asked.

"You really want to?" she whispered. "You don't want to go back to sleep?"

"I'm not sleepy anymore," Jonathan said.

"Me, either," Nick agreed, looking both proud and surprised. "I slept all the way through the night."

"What great news!" Lilah said. "Okay, meet me at the kitchen door and we'll get to work."

They met her so quickly that she wondered if they'd slept in their clothes. Jonathan was wearing shorts that weren't his own. Nor was the oversize T-shirt, which said, Fair Meadows Soccer Camp. Her heart wrenched, but her optimism level steadied almost immediately when she entered the wonderful old kitchen. "Okay, Nick, help me out here. What do you guys usually have for breakfast?"

"We have four different breakfasts." Nick recited them. "Eggs and sausage, pancakes and bacon, oatmeal and toast and French toast with ham."

No cold cereal? "Which is your favorite?"

He sighed. "French toast, but we had that yesterday and ate all the ham."

"Second choice?"

"Scrambled eggs and sausage. J.J., do you like eggs and sausage?"

*J.J.?* She'd ask about that later.

"Oh, yeah," Jonathan said.

She opened the refrigerator. Three dozen eggs. Three wrapped rolls of sausage. She lifted an eyebrow. That should do it. A carton of buttermilk at the back of the shelf gave her a bright idea. "Where's the flour?"

"In here," Nick said.

In the cupboard she found everything she'd need. "Do you like biscuits?"

"Yeah," Nick breathed. "Jesse makes 'em sometimes."

"Okay, we have our menu," she said briskly. "You two can set the table while I'm getting the biscuits started."

Jonathan was cutting out biscuits and Nick was shaping sausage into patties when the door opened and Daniel walked in. His shirt and jeans were filthy. His hair was uncombed, and it seemed to have bits of straw in it. He looked exhausted. "What's going on here?" he asked.

ALL HE'D SAID WAS "what's going on?" But even that scared her. Her feet nearly left the ground.

"Sorry I surprised you." He tried to smooth his hair. "I can see what's going on here. You're cooking breakfast."

Then he took a second look at Lilah. She wasn't the same woman she'd been the night before. Now, she looked clean, fresh and wholesome, well-rested. Pretty. Her hair swung around her shoulders, silky and shining, and her eyes, even bluer than her shirt, looked capable of sparkling. In fact, they probably had been sparkling until he'd walked in.

Lilah gave him a faint smile, then went back to whatever she'd been doing at the sink. Nick had apparently been too excited to sense the tension in the air. "We're making eggs and sausage," he said. "Lilah's making biscuits—and I slept all the way through the night!"

Daniel leaned over to hug him. "I don't know which one of those news flashes is the best one," he said. Looking up at Lilah, he started to wink, then thought better of it.

"Were you in a car wreck?" Jonathan asked.

"Jonathan!" Lilah said.

"I look like it, don't I? But," he sighed, "it was just piglets."

Jonathan swiveled with the biscuit cutter still in his hand, and a raw biscuit plopped onto the floor. "You were attacked by piglets?"

"Of course not!" Lilah reached down for the dough, tossed it in the trash and vigorously scrubbed her hands.

All at once, Daniel felt less tired. "No, I delivered them. Eight of them."

Nick said, "Can we have one?"

"No," Daniel said in synch with another "No!" trumpeted from the hallway. Daniel fell heavily into a kitchen chair and groaned. When Jesse saw his kitchen had been invaded, World War III was likely to break out.

"No pigs in this house," he insisted as he came through the door. "We have enough—" He halted when he took in the scene, and Lilah seemed to tense, as if she were seeing it through Jesse's eyes.

She was whipping eggs. Jonathan was cutting out biscuits. Nick occupied the remaining counter space with his sausage operation. This was *Jesse's* kitchen, *his* biscuit cutter, *his* wire whip. Feeling as tense as Lilah looked, Daniel waited to see how it was all going to come down.

Right before his eyes, she changed. "Jesse," Lilah said, giving him a sunny smile, "I hope it's okay for me to help with breakfast. My goodness. The way you keep this kitchen puts me to shame. I thought I was neat, but your refrigerator is in perfect order, and I found all the biscuit ingredients lined up in the same cupboard, so it didn't take me any time at all to make them. Everything is spotless, and I promise you it will be, well, almost as spotless when we're through."

Daniel nearly let out a whoosh of breath that would have given away his nervousness. Jesse grumbled a little, scraped his foot against the brick floor and said, "The military does that to you. Everything shipshape, you know."

"The military does wonderful things for young men," Lilah responded earnestly. "Teaches them routine, and order, and a sense of responsibility. I could learn a lot from you."

"I'll give you some kitchen management tips when we have some time," Jesse said with the arrogance of a man who's been told he's perfect, which he knew anyway.

Daniel couldn't believe it. The tough marine was melting like butter on a hot griddle. "The boys know," Lilah went on, "that breakfast won't be as good as if you'd cooked it, especially the biscuits, but I wanted to say thank you and this was all I could think of."

"Mighty thoughtful of you," Jesse said. "I have to admit my war injuries are kicking up this morning."

"You got hurt in the war?"

Daniel figured Jonathan's morning was getting off to a pretty exciting start. One man with piglet wounds and another with war wounds. Lilah was left to finish the cooking while Jesse entertained the two boys with a harrowing story of capture and escape due to the heroism of his buddies. Daniel wandered away to his room and made fast work of a shower and a change of clothes. The usual sounds of the morning began to fill the house, the clatter of footsteps, shouting, laughing, barking, and then the barbarian attack on the kitchen.

Joining them, he glanced down at the table. To the left of each place setting was a paper napkin folded into the shape of a pig. Lilah saw his expression. "Origami," she said. "We had a few extra minutes while the biscuits baked." She looked ever so slightly defensive, as if she expected the pigs might make him mad.

"Aw," Daniel said. "You did it in Maggie's honor."

"Maggie?"

"Maggie the sow. You know, instead of cigars, piglet napkins."

She laughed, actually laughed. Her face lit up and her eyes sparkled. "Of course," she said. "Congratulations, Dad."

He hadn't felt this good since—since he'd delivered Maggie's last piglet. It was fine, as all the others had been, and she was fine—which she wouldn't have been if he hadn't helped her out.

*Maggie trusts me. Why doesn't Lilah Jamison?*

The boys were wedged in around the table, Jesse among them—any more boys and Daniel would have to turn this table into an oval—and when he pulled out his chair, he paused, looked around, counted and observed, "We need one more place setting."

"Oh, no," Lilah said. "I have to be running around serving. It's what Jesse did last night…"

"But not what we're doing this morning," Daniel said. "Everybody crunch closer."

TWENTY MINUTES LATER, when not a scrap of food was left anywhere except on the oilcloth and the boys' shirts, Daniel said, "You guys have to get off to soccer camp, and I mean right now."

They were all wearing Fair Meadows Soccer Camp T-shirts. Lilah felt her face flush. "Jonathan and I must be going as soon as we clean up the kitchen."

"Jonathan's going to soccer camp, too," Daniel said.

"Hop to it, men," Jesse barked, moving away from the breakfast table and herding the boys out the door. "Brush your teeth, comb your hair, get your gear."

Three seconds from chaos to silence. Lilah was alone in the kitchen with Daniel. She got up and began to load the dishwasher with lightning speed. "Daniel, Jonathan, unlike every other child in Serenity Valley," she said, cold on the inside and cold on the outside, "isn't signed up for soccer camp."

"Yes, he is," Daniel said. "Last night when I was seeing everybody off to bed Nick reminded me about soccer camp. So I called the coach and registered Jonathan."

She fixed her eyes firmly on the lower dishwasher rack. "Sorry," she said, "but I can't afford it right now."

"I get a group rate," Daniel said, "which I richly deserve, so I told him to add one more to my group."

She swiveled to stare at him. "But he doesn't have the clothes or the shoes…"

Daniel gave her a look that suggested she'd almost exceeded the limits of his patience. "Lilah, we have so many hand-me-downs in the attic we could open a thrift shop. I don't throw anything away until it's a rag, because I never know what size boy might be arriving next. Jonathan is wearing…" He counted on his fingers. "Nick's shorts. The shoes Will outgrew. A shirt of Jason's that got washed in hot water and shrank. We got the gear together last night. So *don't worry.*"

"Okay," she said, turning back to the dishes and registering the stunned silence behind her.

"Okay?"

"What else can I say? I'm sure Jonathan's terribly excited about the camp, and you've dressed him for it. It's out of my hands now."

"Doesn't it feel good for a change?"

"It won't last forever," she said, scrubbing viciously

at a huge frying pan. "Jonathan's expectations have risen, and I can't do the same things for him that you can."

"If you take the job I'm offering, you can."

It was blackmail, pure and simple. What she'd feared last night was becoming a reality. She was falling head-long into Daniel Foster's tender trap.

THE MORE DANIEL THOUGHT about it, the more deter-mined he was to hire Lilah. The carriage house would be all hers. Jonathan could stay there with her or room with Nick. She'd have a salary, plus free room and board. It was a real job—was it ever!—so she'd feel in-dependent financially.

From his point of view, he could keep an eye on her and Jonathan, make sure they were eating enough, know that they had what they needed and that whatever demons were chasing her wouldn't be able to find her. That was all he wanted, to help her get back on her feet.

"No," he heard her say. Her tone was cool. "I know what you're doing, Daniel, but we're not a charity case. I'd like to be your housekeeper, but I need my own place to live. I can't be dependent on you, and frankly, you can't depend on me in the long run." He looked question marks at her. "Churchill is an experiment," she explained. Her voice quavered. "We might have to move on if it doesn't work out."

"Then I'd hire somebody else," he said. "Think about it some more. The boys help with the cleaning, which is why," and he aimed a rueful smile at her rigid back, "the house lacks a certain…polish. That'll give you time to help the kids with homework and Jesse with the cooking. You'd be more like an ordinary mother than a housekeeper. These boys need a mother badly."

She turned to look at him again, thoughtfully. He thought he had her hooked, but the hint of interest in her eyes died as quickly as it had come to life. "I like the boys very much," she said, "but my life is too uncertain right now. I wouldn't want them to become attached to me."

"As I said, just think about it." He wasn't letting her go yet. "In the meantime, will you work for me today, catching up on the laundry? With Jesse so stiff and sore, he can't go up and down the stairs to the basement."

Daniel could see her batting that option back and forth. He was gaming her, which he hated doing. But when he thought about Lilah and Jonathan sleeping in that small car, eating cold food, counting every cent, he couldn't stand it. He couldn't stand to let her do that to her son. Anything he could think of, any lie he had to tell, would be worth it in order to keep her here.

"Well, I suppose I could work for you today. I have the dishes to finish, and I have to wait for Jonathan anyway." She looked at him somewhat hopefully as she rationalized a decision she hadn't wanted to make.

"Jesse will be very grateful. He rarely complains, but…"

She was still gazing at him, the dirty dishes temporarily forgotten. "Some war wounds never completely heal," she said. "I understand they have a certain random quality. For example, one evening a man can leap around a kitchen, cooking dinner for eight people, and the next morning he can hardly move."

Was that a twinkle in her eye or was she being sarcastic? He couldn't tell, and he was afraid to assume anything. He wondered if his face was red, because it felt red. *And* he'd just banged his knee on a table leg. Clumsy as a teenager. "Well, it's time to get those boys off to camp. Come on, guys," he shouted, "time to go."

They came in a platoon, with Jesse lining them up for inspection at the bottom of the stairs. "Okay, Jesse," Daniel called into the hallway. "Load the car and get this show on the road. And buy out the grocery store on the way back."

Jesse really was hobbling when he stepped into the kitchen. In an unsteady voice, he said, "Miss Lilah, do you think you could do the driving? I'm still feeling sort of punk. I'll go along and navigate, and I can help out at the grocery store." He paused for a second, then added, "Help out the best I can, anyway." He offered the keys to her.

What in the heck was he up to? Except for Sunday mornings, when Jesse liked to watch PBS news-in-depth, he wouldn't hand over the keys to that van unless you knocked him down and sat on him. Furthermore, his leg was as fine as it ever would be. The four boys were staring at Jesse as if he'd morphed into an alien. But they weren't saying a word. *Good boys. Keep it up. We have a situation here.*

Lilah put down her scrubbing brush. "I'd be happy to help you, Jesse," she said. "You're sure you feel like going along? The boys probably know where the camp is."

"Of course I feel like going along," Jesse snapped, apparently forgetting his new persona. "Don't think I should be driving these kids, though, with my shaky leg and all." He'd segued directly back into the frail old-man voice.

"Then let's go," Lilah said, and headed for the carriage house where the van was parked.

Daniel had to sit down again. It was as if they all knew; as if they were all helping him out. And then he thought, *What is it exactly they're helping me out with?*

*Maybe they're helping themselves out, already imagining her as a mother figure and liking the idea.*

He pulled himself together. He had a full schedule today, including a trip out to the Edwards farm to give the Jersey milk cows a thorough examination. This evening he had a meeting that was important to him— one that could shape the rest of his life.

"WE GOT HERE FIRST!" Nick shouted.

They'd reached a tree-fenced field on the outskirts of Churchill. A stocky man, obviously the coach, waved when he saw the van. "Bye, Mom," Jonathan said. He leaned over the seat to give her a hug. *I'm being dragged into all of this because of Jonathan,* she thought before she reached behind her to return the hug. "Show them your stuff, Tiger," she said.

The boys sped off to meet the coach, who greeted them warmly with high-fives and manly punches to their shoulders, acting as if he couldn't think of anything he'd rather do on a beautiful summer day than play soccer with a bunch of kids. More cars arrived. Moms, already looking tired in their shorts or work clothes, and dads looking proud, waved their carloads of boys and girls onto the field.

Lilah watched, seeing Jonathan mix right in with the others, and couldn't help feeling a glow of happiness. At the same time she was thinking, *not for long.*

Jesse said, "Wish I could run like those boys. Can't even walk fast anymore. And this morning…"

"Jesse," Lilah said, turning a direct glance on him, "I know when I'm being worked on. So cut it out. We're going to hit that grocery store like an attack force. I have laundry to do." But then she smiled at him, enjoying the sheepish look on his face.

JESSE PUT THE GROCERIES away while Lilah stared at the laundry piled beneath and around an old-fashioned clothes chute. She'd never been in the back of a professional laundry, but she couldn't imagine that even one of them would have so many dirty clothes on hand. Mountains of them. Mixed in with sheets, towels—she half expected to find a dead body in there.

The washer and dryer were huge. She filled the washer with many sheets as she dared to and started the first load. While they washed, she'd sort the rest of the laundry.

Darks, lights, whites, towels, more sheets. Flinging the items into one pile or another, she came across the tan plaid shirt Daniel had been wearing when he came home from delivering the piglets. For a moment she held it in her hands, fingering the soft fabric, as scenes of Daniel and his boys danced through her mind. She pressed it to her face, taking in the manly smell of soap, warm skin and straw. Then she quickly tossed it into the "lights" pile. There was something all too comfortable about Daniel. She'd told him she didn't want the boys to have time to become attached to her. But she didn't want to get attached to them, either. And even more importantly, she didn't want to become attached to Daniel or vulnerable to his opinion of her. Or vulnerable to any other man, ever again.

AT ELEVEN-THIRTY SHE started another load of washing, then went upstairs to the kitchen. Aengus stared at Jesse with rapt attention as he piled something onto hamburger buns, dozens of them. "Hot tuna salad sandwiches," he explained. "For lunch. The guys love them."

"I'll be on my way to pick them up," Lilah said.

"*I* pick them up," Jesse said, sounding sort of huffy, and then he caught himself in his own trap. "I mean," he said, shuffling his feet, "I'm feeling a lot better now."

"I'm *so* glad to hear it." She shot him a sidelong glance. "I was terribly worried about you."

He glared at her. She smiled back. "So I'll just go on with the laundry."

A half hour later, silence exploded into chaos above her head. Ah, the boys were home. Almost immediately, footsteps thumped down the stairs to the basement. "Mom," Jonathan said, "we practiced making goals, and I made more than anybody my age!"

She dropped the towel she was folding and gave him a hug. "You are the best soccer player ever."

While she was at his level, he whispered in her ear, "I even made more than Will, but don't tell him I told you."

"Not a word," she said, "but that's really something. He must be...ten, maybe?"

"He's eleven," Jonathan hissed.

"Wow!" Now she had to bring him back down to earth. "Honey, we were going back to our hideout when you got home, but I said I'd stay today and do the laundry."

"Good," Jonathan said, "because after lunch everybody goes to the pool."

Lilah sighed. The tender trap tightened around her every moment Jonathan spent in its embrace. "Okay," she said. "Run over to the carriage house and get the sunscreen out of my bag. Your swimsuit's in the car."

"Nick's loaning me a swimsuit," Jonathan said, "but I don't know about the sunscreen. You coming upstairs for lunch?"

"Well, I—"

"Lilah," Jesse shouted down the stairs, "lunch in ten minutes!"

"I guess I am," she said.

Jonathan paused at the bottom of the steep basement stairs. "Mom," he said hesitantly, "did you get the job?"

"Dr. Foster offered me the job," she said carefully, "but it might not be quite right for me."

"I really hope you take it," he said. "I like it here."

His steps were slow as he climbed the stairs. Lilah sank her face into her hands. What was she going to do?

IT WAS CLOSE TO FOUR O'CLOCK when Jesse yelled down at her again. "You don't have to bring up the clothes," he said. "Everybody gets his own."

She was, at that moment, wearily heading for the kitchen cradling a basket in each arm, wondering if Jesse had ever been able to negotiate those stairs or if Daniel and the boys had been trying to manage the laundry themselves. "Thank goodness," she moaned. She dropped the basket onto the kitchen table. "Here are the dish towels and cloths," she said. "I'll take up the sheets and bath towels and leave everything else. I had no idea what belonged to whom. Can the boys figure it out?"

Jesse turned away from a steaming pot that was giving out a delicious smell of tomatoes, garlic and basil. "They pick things up by size," he said. "Somehow it all works out. I bet you could use something to drink before the mob gets home. Lemonade?"

"Sounds wonderful. Jesse, do you think Daniel would mind if I used the computer in the living room for a few minutes?"

"Of course not. I'm off to the pool, so enjoy the peace and quiet while you can."

Lilah took the glass of lemonade he handed her, cold, tart and delicious, and sat down at the computer. In a few minutes she was into the Web site of *The Kingdom Dispatch,* the weekly newspaper that served Whittaker and the rest of the Northeast Kingdom, reading the news clips.

The city council was fighting again, this time over a new truck for the volunteer fire department. The principal of the elementary school had resigned.

But those newsy tidbits weren't what Lilah was looking for. She stiffened. There on the screen was Bruce's face, a study in remorse. "Bruce Jamison was recently released from Northeast State Correctional Facility after serving three years of his five-year sentence. 'He's been a model prisoner,' says Prison Supervisor Lex Holt. 'We feel he's ready to return to his community and live a useful life.'"

"Right," Lilah muttered, "a useful life." She read on, feeling more disgusted by the minute.

"In a recent interview, Jamison expressed his regret to God, the community and his family. 'I don't know what made me do it,' he said. 'I'm not the kind of person to take good money from hardworking folks. While I was getting my mind straight in prison, I realized I was glad they caught me so that those folks could get their money back.'"

Not all of it, however. Lilah had had to make up the rest, and doing so had left her penniless.

"'I feel the worst about my family. My wife and my son have left me, and I understand why. But I'm going to move heaven and earth to find them and try to win back their love and respect. If anybody knows their whereabouts, I would appreciate the information.'"

*Her flesh crawled. He will find us. He'll punish me for the rest of my life for turning him in. And Jonathan... Jonathan...*

Her hands were icy as she acknowledged the truth: There was no safe place for her and Jonathan.

She got up from the computer and stared at Daniel's homey, untidy living room. Unless it was here. Even if Daniel wasn't quite as great a guy as he seemed to be, they'd still be safer here than they would be running from Bruce at his most determined. Maybe it was the only choice she had.

The house suddenly filled with noise, and above all the boys' voices she could hear Daniel's. "How many goals? Good grief, Jonathan, I'm harboring a celebrity. Yes, I mean you."

Lilah could imagine the scene in the kitchen. Daniel would ruffle Jonathan's hair, give him that infectious grin, and Jonathan would beam back. She closed the Web site and stepped into the kitchen.

While Jason and Maury stood back, looking indulgent when they meant to look bored, the younger boys gave Daniel a blow-by-blow description of their day, surrounding him like adoring fans. Then, at Jesse's suggestion—command was more like it—they flooded into the basement, returning with armloads of clothes and calling, "Thanks, Lilah," as they raced away to their rooms.

She felt exhausted but she had something to say, and she had to say it now, before she lost her nerve. While Jesse was microwaving popcorn, she said quietly to Daniel, "May I talk to you a minute? In private?"

He stepped into the hall with her. He looked worried, which made her feel more determined to get it over with. She drew in a deep breath. "Daniel, if your job offer's still open, I'll accept it."

# Chapter Four

Daniel was elated to have the housekeeper search over and done with, even though the way Lilah had accepted the job made him think she might just as well have been saying to her doctor, "Yes, I'll have the spinal fusion. Without anesthetic." And after delivering the message, she'd fled so quickly that he hadn't even had time to talk to her about her salary.

Why did he make her so nervous? He could understand that she wouldn't want to become involved with anyone so soon after losing her husband, but hell, he wasn't asking her to get involved. He'd only been trying to give her a job that included room and board! He hadn't flirted with her and asking her to have dinner in the kitchen with his family and his dog surely couldn't be confused with asking her for a date. It had been her own idea to interview for the job; she needed one desperately, and he'd practically had to force it on her. What was her problem?

Even if she was somewhat neurotic, however, he felt he'd made a good decision. Jonathan was his proof that she'd be good to the boys, which was all that mattered. Shaking his head, he wandered back into the clinic, where he'd have a brief window of time in which to think about the meeting of the Serenity Valley Regional Development Board this evening. There he planned to bring up some new business, the dream he'd been cherishing for the past several years.

Taking in foster children had made him a whole man again, but there was a limit to the number of kids he could handle on his own. And in Vermont there were dozens, maybe even hundreds of children going hungry, being neglected, some of them being physically abused, as well. He could do more by himself, but not enough.

On fifteen acres of Ian's sheep farm in Holman, the town at the tip of the valley, he wanted to build a foster care center to meet the needs of several dozen children. He'd already consulted an architect and talked to some government agencies and private foundations about funding. Daniel felt ready to test the waters.

He was thinking about what he'd say at the meeting when Mildred appeared in the doorway. "Betty brought Tiffany in with a sore paw," she whispered. "Can you take a minute to see her?"

Daniel groaned. "Sure," he said. "A sore paw could be fatal."

"How's business?" Ian Foster stuck his head through the door of Daniel's examination room.

"Steady, as you can see." His current patient, a giant Maine coon cat, glared balefully at Ian.

"Don't look at me," Ian growled. "He's the one who's sticking the needle into your—"

"Language," Daniel said automatically.

"Hey, it's me," Ian said. "I'm in charge of my own language."

"Okay, Tiffany, you're all set," Daniel said to the cat.

"Tiffany?"

"I don't get to name the patients, Ian, I just get to stick needles into them. Tiffany's good to go," he called out into the waiting room.

"Why isn't Tiffany's owner in here with her in her time of trial?" Ian rolled his eyes as he said the cat's name.

"These," Daniel said, pulling off a pair of gloves a steelworker might find adequate. "We don't want Tiffany's mom to know that her kitty is one of the most vicious…Betty! Here she is. Her paw's going to be fine."

The stout gray-haired woman swept the cat into her arms and said, "Ooh, was Mommy's little precious a good girl for Dr. Foster? Of course you were, you little sweetums."

Ian looked as if he might upchuck. The woman bustled out, carrying the cat, who was purring now, upside down in her arms like a baby. Mike, the middle Foster brother, came in in her wake, carrying takeout containers in much the same way Betty had carried the cat. "Dinner," he said succinctly. "It'll be a long, tough meeting. We need fortification."

"You don't have to be at the restaurant?"

"It'll be fine. Almost everybody ate early anyway.

My guess is they're all going to the meeting. I dropped off last night's leftovers at the house, too."

"You don't want to eat last night's leftovers with the kids?"

"Not tonight. Seems the table would be too full." Mike narrowed his eyes. "Who was that vision of beauty in the kitchen with Jesse who ran like a gazelle as soon as she saw me?"

Ian gave Mike a long, contemplative look, then turned his gaze on Daniel.

Daniel hadn't thought of her as a "vision of beauty," but now that Mike mentioned it, she had cleaned up well. "That's Lilah Jamison," he said, feeling uneasy. "She's, well, she's my new housekeeper. I told you about the housekeeper, and you agreed I needed some help…"

"We agreed you needed a housekeeper," Mike said. "I was expecting a different sort of person."

"What do you know about her?" Ian said.

"She's a widow."

His brothers waited for more. "Where does she come from?" Mike asked.

"I don't know. We haven't talked that much."

Ian and Mike stared at each other. "Where'd you find her—or *vice versa?*" Ian chimed in.

Daniel sighed. "She saw my ad and asked for an interview. She has a son, six or seven years old. I finally figured out they were homeless. I turned the job into one for a live-in housekeeper."

"Omigod," Ian moaned. "Don't tell me. She said, 'Oh, my, I just don't know, but, well, yes, I can do that.'"

"I had to con her into accepting the job," Daniel snapped. "They've been living in their car, and I have an empty apartment. And besides, Nick met her son at Sunday school, they hit it off, and she made Nick a dreamcatcher."

"A what?" Ian said, scowling.

"It's a thing. A totem. A good luck charm. Wards off bad dreams." He took off his lab coat, washed his hands and gestured both of them into the waiting room.

Mike lined up the carry-out cartons on the receptionist's counter and started heaping food onto plastic plates. Beef cooked in wine, some fancy kind of scalloped potatoes, asparagus, crusty bread.

"Looks great," Daniel said enthusiastically. "What do you call those potatoes? And is this the daube or the bourguignonne?"

"Don't change the subject. Have you moved her into the house?"

"The carriage house. Before she even agreed to take the job, she cooked breakfast, did the laundry…"

Mike and Ian gave each other another one of those irritating looks. This was a common occurrence, but Daniel liked it much better when he and one of them was giving the third one that look. Ian settled himself in a seat against the wall, and Daniel sat down a chair away for elbow room. Mike chose a spot facing Daniel. Plate in hand, he said, "Daniel."

"What?" Daniel replied, knowing what was coming and already feeling cross.

"Do you remember the dog you brought home just before you were going off to vet school, when we were waiting to close out our jobs? The one who ripped up the kitchen floor? Which the landlord made Ian and me replace, when we were living on spaghetti *without* meatballs? Sometimes without sauce?"

"You did good things with spaghetti," Ian said. "A little oil, some cheese…"

"Shut up, Ian. We're not talking about my cooking."

"It wasn't the dog's fault," Daniel protested. "He missed me. You brought him with you when we joined up again, and he was the best dog…"

"And that girl," Ian said, "also homeless, who moved in with us and left with every penny of the paychecks we'd just cashed?"

"That disappointed me," Daniel said. "She'd had a terrible life, though, and—"

"The old man selling magazine subscriptions?"

"Mike, every family should subscribe to a high-quality news magazine—"

"And every old man should have a good hot meal—a twenty-dollar good hot meal. Daniel," Mike said, "you're doing it again. You're taking in another stray."

"Lilah? She's nothing like that girl we took in. She's a good person who needs a break."

"How can you tell she's a good person?" Mike asked. "How much time have you spent with her? Thirty minutes?"

"I can tell from her son. They're crazy about each other. He's a homeless kid who feels sure his mom can turn things around. And," he added, "say what you want to about dreamcatchers, but Nick didn't have any nightmares last night."

"Well, that's something," Mike said. "All it took was a dreamcatcher."

Daniel and his brothers were always honest with each other. "And her son, Jonathan, spending the night. That probably had more to do with it than the dreamcatcher."

"Great," Ian said. "They probably stayed up all night throwing pillows at each other. No time for nightmares."

"He's a great kid," Daniel insisted. "He went to soccer camp with the kids this morning and they said he…"

"You paid for him to go to soccer camp."

"I couldn't let him feel left out. Look, you two," Daniel said, fed up with his brothers' doubts. "She's lost her husband. She has a scar on her forehead. I can't put it all together yet, but something bad has happened to this woman. She's not the kind of person you'd ever expect to be homeless and penniless. I just want to help her, that's all."

For a second he thought they were going to jump him and wrestle him to the ground. Not that they really would, but they looked as if they'd like to. He stood up. "Great dinner, Mike. We have a few minutes before the meeting. So come meet her—officially, I mean. And act nice," he said, glaring at them.

WHEN A MAN ABOUT Daniel's height, but somehow *bigger,* had walked into the kitchen without knocking, Lilah instinctively fled, even though she was supposed to be tossing a salad to go with Jesse's lasagna. *Who is he?* In the few minutes she heard him talking to Jesse, he'd sounded like a stand-up comedian.

At last she sneaked downstairs to finish the salad. At the bottom of the staircase, she became aware of footsteps and voices coming from the clinic. It was too late to flee again. Daniel and his companions had spotted her.

"Lilah Jamison," Daniel said, "meet my brothers, Mike and Ian."

The hallway was crammed with Fosters, tall, imposing Fosters: Mike, the one who'd come into the kitchen without knocking, and the third one, who glared at her as if he disliked her even before he'd met her. She was trapped. She held out a shaky hand to each of them.

"I'm Ian."

The one who glared.

"Mike," said Mike. His smile was guarded, as if he was testing her.

Lilah tried to take them in. Mike was a little taller than Daniel, and Ian, a little shorter. While Daniel had sandy hair and light-brown eyes—Ian's hair was dark, as were his eyes, both dark and brooding. Mike's head was shaved, but his red-brown eyebrows and faint freckling gave him away. A redhead with spectacular green eyes.

She took a second look. "You don't look anything alike," she blurted out, then realized they might have been adopted. She blushed. "Oh, I'm so sorry. I shouldn't have said that."

"We get that a lot," Daniel said quickly, probably to fill the sudden silence. "And we're pretty darned grateful for it. Aren't we?" he added, when the other two remained silent.

"Uh-huh," Mike murmured, staring at Lilah. Ian, on the other hand, just kept glaring.

"Well," Lilah said, feeling dismissed, "I'm glad I got to meet you."

The brothers muttered something that might have been "nice to meet you, too," and then Ian said, "We're late for a meeting." His voice was steely.

But Daniel smiled at her. "Everything under control here?"

"Absolutely," she said, afraid to smile back. "Don't worry about a thing."

When they left, she collapsed on the stairs. The two brothers Daniel hadn't mentioned didn't like her. Didn't want her here. She'd had no idea Daniel had brothers who might have a say in his hiring her. Fearing that Bruce would find her, she'd made a commitment to Daniel, to Jonathan, to Jesse and to Daniel's boys.

But her most important commitment was to herself and Jonathan. If his brothers didn't like her, how would Daniel come to feel about her? And if he began to dislike her, to regret his job offer, might she and Jonathan find themselves living in close proximity with and dependent upon a man like Bruce? She'd leave now, with Jonathan, before it could fall down on her.

"Mom!" In the dimly lit hall, Jonathan barreled into her on his way out of the kitchen. "Guess what? We're having lasagna for dinner, and Uncle Mike brought all kinds of pies! Jesse says we can have them for dessert."

Already, the enemy was "Uncle Mike." Lilah sighed, then joined Jesse in the kitchen to finish dressing the salad.

AFTER A BRIEF ARGUMENT, Mike got to drive and Ian copped the front seat. Daniel compressed himself into the backseat of Mike's Subaru wagon. "Ian, you could at least move your seat forward," he grumbled.

"What the hell's wrong with you?" Ian asked as soon as they were on their way to the Town Hall for the meeting. "Taking that woman in without checking her out."

Daniel knew his brothers were just trying to protect him, but he was an adult now and able to protect himself. "I asked Child Services to check her out," he snapped. "She has a great kid, she has Jesse kissing her feet, and the boys seem to want her around."

"So now you're letting the boys choose the housekeeper?"

"I've learned to trust people, okay? A skill you could stand to work on."

"Time out!" Mike said. "We all need to calm down here. Daniel, you can't get mad. How this meeting goes tonight will affect the rest of your life, and you won't do it right if you're mad. So," and now he raised his voice, "if you guys can't stop fighting in the car, Mom and I aren't taking you to Disneyland next summer."

A brief silence, then Daniel chuckled. A second later, Ian snorted. He turned around in the car seat. "I was counting on Disneyland," he said, his voice and his face as gruff as ever.

"So pull yourself together for the meeting, Daniel," Mike said.

"Don't worry. Five minutes of sulking and I'll be in top form." He had to be. His project, his dream, meant too much to him. He couldn't blow off this chance to do something really important, to protect more children than he could possibly fit into his house on Prospect Street.

DISCUSSION AT THE MEETING droned on forever. It was an open board meeting, which meant all Serenity Valley residents could attend, but Daniel still couldn't imagine why so many of them had come out. He fidgeted in his seat, waiting for the words, "The floor is now open for new business."

If anybody took the floor before he did, he thought the veins in his temples might explode.

The moment arrived, and he shot from his seat. "Mr. Chairman."

"Daniel. Yes." The chairman of the board gave him a nod. "State your name, please, and present your business."

He stated his name as requested, although everybody in the room already knew who he was, and then he began his pitch, trying to sound easy and casual. "Most of you know I take in foster children," he began. "And that has gotten me interested in the whole foster home situation." He went on, respectful of those who already were foster parents, but emphasizing the number of children who probably needed foster care and weren't getting it.

"Many communities," and he named various other places, "have built foster-care centers designed to house a number of children in individual homes staffed by couples, with common rooms in a larger main building that would also house…"

The local pediatrician was nodding. So was the head

of Child Services in the valley. On the other hand, the Churchill minister's wife, Virginia Galloway, was frowning, and several members of the Women's Auxiliary had their heads together with hers. Daniel was sure she was a good person—she taught the teenagers' Sunday school class and she hadn't expelled Jason or Maury yet—but he'd never been able to work up much enthusiasm for the woman. Ironically, he was probably going to have to persuade these godly women to be kind to others who were less fortunate, while the inebriated man who'd staggered into a backseat at the last minute would turn out to be 100 percent in favor of the project.

"My brother Ian has volunteered to donate land for the project, if it receives your approval. The kids will have playing fields to share with the rest of the valley, and a safe, protected environment. I've consulted an architect, and I've researched the grants that might be available. But I'll need your support to move on to the planning stage, and I'd like to hear your opinions."

"The floor is open for discussion," the chairman said.

When the minister's wife raised her hand, Daniel's heart sank. The chairman acknowledged her, and she asked, "Would any of these children come from locations outside the valley?"

"Yes," Daniel said politely. "The facility would be available to any child in Vermont."

"Aren't you at all concerned that this foster center would bring undesirable elements into the valley?"

Daniel was gritting his teeth to keep from snapping, "No," when he heard Ian's voice. Startled looks came from the audience. Ian wasn't noted for contributing verbally to any cause.

"Ian?" the chairman said doubtfully.

Daniel held his breath. If Ian spoke the way he usually did, it could mean the end of the center. His gruffness and reserve put people off. God knew what he might say. The townspeople should focus on what he's done, Daniel worried, donating that land, and not what he... And then his eyes widened. Was that calm, even voice Ian's?

"Ma'am," Ian said, directing his gaze toward the minister's wife. "With all due respect, we're not talking about 'elements' here, we're talking about children."

Daniel was gratified to hear a ripple of laughter run through the room.

"The children aren't undesirable. Is any child undesirable?" He pinned his gaze on the woman, who shifted in her seat.

"Many of the parents of these children aren't undesirable, either," Ian went on. "They're poverty-stricken, or they're sick, or one parent is fine but the other is abusive. Sometimes the parents really care about their children, but they know they can't afford to take care of them."

Just as abruptly as he'd stood up, Ian sat down.

Daniel was stunned. He'd never heard Ian speak so eloquently. He'd never heard him speak eloquently at all.

The pediatrician, who was legendary for his lack of tact in situations not involving his patients, leapt to his feet. "Don't be an idiot, Virginia," he said to the minister's wife. "As Foster said, the children aren't criminals. Just because they're foster children doesn't mean they're going to raise hell."

"The sins of the fathers are visited on the children," intoned the minister from the back of the room.

He and his wife were a perfect couple.

"The sins of the fathers, speaking generically," the head of Child Services spoke up, "often result in the need for foster homes for the children. In that sense I agree with you."

Other objections arose, along with other statements in defense of the project. Daniel felt exhausted, and now, as if Mike were tuned in to his thought process, he raised his hand.

"Daniel's been talking to Ian and me about this project for a long time," he told the group in his smiling, easygoing way, "so I'm not exactly objective."

The group smiled back at him. Of the three of them, Daniel thought dolefully, Mike did the best job of fitting in with the community. Nothing like having the best restaurant—the only real restaurant—in the valley. People had a vested interest in staying on his good side.

"But I do think you folks need to know more specifics. Mr. Chairman, I'd like to propose that Daniel deliver a formal presentation with all the details at the next board meeting."

In seconds, the chairman had a motion and a second from the floor, and the show of hands was impressive. Apparently the townspeople wanted to know about the center, at least.

Daniel's heart swelled with affection for Mike and

Ian. Whatever their disagreements, their bond stood firm. All for one, one for all.

"WELL, NOT A COUP," Mike said on the way home, "but a good start. Virginia Galloway lost this one."

"We need a mole in the Women's Auxiliary," Ian growled. "Or a hit man."

"I'd prefer the mole," Daniel said.

"You would," Ian said.

"Disneyland?" Mike said.

"Okay," Daniel said. "When we get back to my place we're all going in to see if Lilah has bruised, mutilated or killed the boys, and then we'll come to an agreement about whether she's a suitable housekeeper." He waited through the silence.

"Okay, fair enough," Mike said.

Daniel released a deep breath. *Dear God, let everything be okay.* Because Mike and Ian were the constants in his life. If they disapproved of Lilah, he couldn't let her stay.

When all three of them had finally set out on their careers, Ian had taken the legal steps to incorporate them. They'd struggled to educate each other in their chosen fields, and following that they'd decided to share the wealth, such as it was. Their income went into a corporate account, out of which they paid themselves equal salaries. Hiring Lilah didn't represent a cost for Daniel alone, but for all three of them.

And maybe Daniel's brothers were right. Maybe he'd taken this trust thing too far.

## Chapter Five

"The house is too dark," Ian said, as Mike pulled into the parking area.

"Not the living room," Daniel remarked. "I imagine they're all in there."

"Tied up," Ian suggested. "Begging for their lives."

"Ian!" Mike said.

"Oh, okay, but I think we ought to sneak in and catch her at whatever she's doing."

"All right," Daniel said, getting out of the car. "Come on." He was sure everything was fine. Had to be. It would be, wouldn't it? Sure it would.

Through the window he saw Lilah standing in the living room, wearing an evil expression. "What the hell—"

She rushed toward the sofa with her arms outstretched. He launched into a run, with his brothers breathing down his neck, and almost ripped the front door off its hinges. As he lunged through the foyer and into the room, he heard a scream, then Jesse said from the far corner, tilting his chair forward and almost falling out of it, "What the heck are you doing, Daniel? You scared us out of our wits."

Daniel came to a stop so suddenly that Mike and Ian rear-ended him. It was Lilah who had screamed, and now she seemed to be breathing hard and trying to pull herself together. Jonathan clung to her. The boys simply stared at Daniel.

"Well," he said to Lilah, reluctant to look her in the eye, "we were coming in from the car, and I saw you, um, rush forward, looking…"

He sent another glance toward the sofa, where the boys were lined up, all perfectly fine and still staring at him. Bowls of popcorn sat on either end of the coffee table, and in the middle was a low, spreading bouquet of heavy white blossoms picked from the snowball bushes that hedged his property.

He didn't think he had any vases. He took a closer look. The container was Jesse's sacred bean pot.

Then he took a look around the rest of the room. Jesse had relaxed back into the rocker, his cane resting against the wall, and Aengus was lying on the round rag rug, standing guard. The room was neater than he'd ever seen it. The wide planks of the maple floor, original to the house, looked funny. They gleamed. Had someone scrubbed them?

"We were playing charades," Jonathan said, "and Mom was acting out the Wicked Witch of the West."

"From *The Wizard of Oz*," Will said, as if Daniel might have missed out on it.

Behind him, Daniel heard a snicker. He'd remind his

brothers later that they were the ones who'd gotten him stirred up.

"I thought it might make a nice change from television and computer games," Lilah said. Her face was pale, but she'd recovered enough to glare at him.

"When we did *Pirates of the Caribbean*," Nick added, "Jason was trying to show us the ocean making waves and..." he began laughing "he fell over."

"The waters were rough," Jason said.

"Want to play?" Will asked.

"Sure!" Mike said.

"I guess so," Ian growled. "What do I have to do?"

"It's nine o'clock," Lilah said. "I believe that's bedtime."

Daniel exchanged a look with her. He tried to tell her with his eyes how stupid he felt, how sorry he was. "I think we can bend the rules once in a while," he said. "It's summertime, and there's nothing I like better than seeing Ian and Mike make fools of themselves."

Her slight smile was almost like forgiveness. When Mike and Ian launched into the game, he did, too. He had a feeling they'd changed their minds about Lilah.

TALK ABOUT BENDING THE rules, it was almost eleven when Daniel sent the boys up to bed and walked Mike and Ian to their cars. The fun hadn't ended when the game was finished. Jesse had brought out wedges of the pies Mike had brought, lemon and chocolate meringue, coconut cream and something absolutely delicious called key lime pie. It was a first for Lilah, and it embarrassed her to realize she'd eaten two pieces of it.

While they ate until nothing was left but crumbs of crust, which Will picked off the serving plate with a finger he'd licked, Daniel, his brothers and the kids engaged in lively conversation about everything under the sun, politics and soccer, recycling and movie ratings, the culinary arts and baseball. Lilah saw how Jonathan entered into the discussion and had clearly been accepted, even celebrated, and it made her feel warm inside.

But the boys were in bed now, even Jonathan, who was having a ball being with other boys, knowing she was a shout away. She and Daniel were alone, and for the first time she didn't feel like running away.

"I'm sorry I freaked out," he said as soon as the house was quiet. "I have this overprotective streak."

"Your entrance was a little overdramatic, I have to admit."

"I should go into show business?"

"I said *over*dramatic." She couldn't understand why she felt comfortable enough to tease him. "Daniel…"

He'd been headed toward the door, but he turned back.

"I know you're exhausted," she said, "but sometime I wish you'd tell me about each of the boys. It would help me know what they need from me."

"What about right now?" Daniel said, although she could see that he was drained to the core by the tensions of the evening. "We should have a glass of Jesse's cooking wine and unwind."

She feigned horror. "You'd veer from the Saturday-night beer and have a glass of wine? Off schedule?"

"I have to save that beer for Saturday night. And besides, my whole household is off schedule."

"You have a point. I'd love a glass of wine."

He came back with wine and gestured toward the empty bowl of popcorn. "Wine and snacks," he said. "How good are your teeth? We seem to have a few unpopped corns left."

"My teeth are excellent, but I've had so much pie I could care less about any more snacks."

He joined her on the sofa. "Before we talk about the boys, I have something for you." He handed her a cell phone.

Lilah shook her head and tried to return it. "Thanks, but no."

Daniel wouldn't take it back. "You might need it. I put you on the family plan, so it won't be expensive. But you should be reachable in an emergency."

She looked at him, then at the phone. Finally, she nodded. "Okay. Thanks."

"Now, about the boys." He settled back on the sofa. "Starting with the oldest, Jason's family lived in an abandoned school bus out in the woods, where his father was growing marijuana. His idea," and Daniel's jaw tightened as he explained this, "was that Jason could deliver the pot. Who's going to be suspicious of a twelve-year-old kid on a bike?"

Lilah moaned. "Horrible," she murmured. "How could a parent do something like that?"

"Well, the parent could, but the son couldn't. When Jason refused to make the deliveries, his father kicked him out of the house. He lived on the street for a year before a social worker caught up with him and put him into foster care. Two other families gave up on him before he came to me. He was mad at the whole world."

"I wouldn't have believed it," she said. "He's kind and helpful, and he has a wonderful, dry sense of humor…"

"And he's a big brother to the younger kids. So's Maury," Daniel went on, "whose past is even more tragic. His parents moved, and moved and moved again, trying to escape their debts. To his mother's credit, she kept him in school—he was in fourteen schools in eight years, never knew where he'd be the next day. One day his dad just fell apart and shot Maury's mom and then himself."

Lilah wondered how she'd ever thought her life had been hard. Her family had been poor, but that was all. Her heart bled for these boys.

"Mike's the one who turned Maury around," Daniel said. "Maury's a born foodie, just like Mike. He spends every minute he can at Mike's restaurant, and as soon as he can drive himself, Mike will give him a regular part-time job. We're bringing up a chef here."

"Do these boys have any idea how lucky they are to be with you?" Her face felt hot. She shouldn't have said something so personal. "I mean," she stammered, "they have you, and Jesse's just like a grandfather, and your brothers are great with them—" She halted suddenly. Her only hope was to change the subject immediately. "Tell me about the other two boys."

"Quick sketches," Daniel said and swallowed a yawn. "Will's parents want him back as soon as they've recovered from really bad injuries in a car accident.

And Nick…" His brow furrowed. "Nick's the most complicated case I have."

He rested his forehead in his hand. "Apparently he was abandoned—or maybe he ran away. All he'll say is that he can't remember where he comes from. I can't stand thinking what those nightmares must have been about."

He got to his feet and looked down at her. When he spoke, his voice was soft. "You've done more for him with that dreamcatcher you made than I've been able to do in the last three months. I'm very grateful."

Lilah stood up, too. "I'm so glad it helped."

When she turned toward him, he suddenly seemed too close. She could see his fatigue, the shadow of a blond beard on his cheeks and a vulnerability in his eyes she hadn't noticed before.

Why should he feel vulnerable to anything? He and his brothers had obviously had happy childhoods, Daniel was well-off, and she suspected Mike and Ian were, too. What did Daniel have to be sad about?

And what was it about him that made her feel drawn to him instinctively, just as Jonathan was?

"One more thing," she said. "The kids are calling Jonathan J.J. It's okay, but I just wondered…"

"We're big on nicknames around here," he said, smile lines crinkling around his eyes. "It sort of says we're all buddies, so everybody has a nickname. Except Jason," he added, as if he were realizing it for the first time.

"And you."

Their gazes locked. He opened his mouth, but before he could say anything, a voice shouted, "Daniel!"

It was Jonathan's voice, and he'd called for Daniel, not for her. Daniel was already moving, Lilah on his heels, when Jonathan spoke again. "Nick's got a splinter in his hand. A big one."

Daniel turned at the door and gave her a crooked grin. "Can you get home okay? I have to make one of those late-night house calls."

"DANIEL, DO YOU HAVE a minute?"

Daniel was attending to a Jack Russell terrier, the beloved pet of Reverend and Mrs. Galloway. He slid a needle into the little dog's plump haunch and allowed himself a moment of self-congratulation—this was the goosiest dog in the world and he didn't even flinch—then looked up to see Dana Holstead standing in his doorway. "Dana!" he said. "Come on in. I always have time for you."

Dana, the head of Child Services in the valley, had been his first real friend in Churchill and also the woman who'd examined every nook and cranny of his character before changing his life by allowing him to become a foster parent. In her fifties and childless, she took each child who came into the Child Services system as a personal responsibility.

"I can't find anything negative about Lilah Jamison," Dana said. "How's she working out?"

It was Dana's job to be interested. Daniel probed the dog's body for cysts and otherwise painful areas and said, "Great so far. Come to dinner next weekend and check her out."

"How is Banjo?" asked Virginia Galloway, sailing

through the door like a ship's figurehead, her substantial bosom leading the way. Apparently, she'd milked Mildred of all her gossip at last.

"In perfect health," Daniel said, thinking to himself that the dog was pampered, overfed and yet, somehow, as overactive as any other Jack Russell.

"Of course he is," Virginia replied, then turned to direct a critical gaze toward Dana and an accusing one toward Daniel. "Dana," she said without much warmth.

"Virginia," Dana said with considerable warmth. "How nice to run into you. Banjo is such a darling."

Dana wasn't a gushy person. If she was pandering to Virginia Galloway, she must have an agenda. "How old is he now?" she went on.

"Fourteen," Virginia said.

"I would have guessed he was just a puppy!"

Had Virginia thawed at all? Daniel couldn't tell. She swept regally from the room, almost certainly on her way to protest the amount of her bill.

"Lovely person," Dana said.

"Salt of the earth," Daniel replied.

"You think she could stall the foster center?"

"Absolutely. She has enormous power in the community. I can't imagine why."

"What can we do about her, short of rat poison?"

"I don't know. You did your best to soften her up, and it didn't work."

"We have to find her weak spot."

"Good luck." Daniel felt gloomy about the prospect.

"Okay, now the good news. I got a letter today—three former foster children who've grown up and done well want to launch a fund-raising effort for your center."

He suddenly felt great. "That makes my day. Looks like our financial prospects are pretty good."

"Hailed from without, condemned from within," Dana said dramatically.

"A prophet without honor in his own country," Daniel intoned.

Dana snickered, then began to fill Daniel in on the details of the offer. Suddenly, she seemed to hear the barking and yowling coming from the waiting room, and the raucous squawk of the poetry-quoting parrot, Robert Frost, Bob for short, named for the famous Vermont poet. The bird had an impressive repertoire of his poems. Even now Bob was screeching, "And miles to go before I sleep."

"Sorry," she said. "I forgot you had a job. Gotta run before Bob Frost launches into 'Birches.'"

"This looks great, Jesse."

"Tell Lilah. She cooked it." But Jesse was beaming like a proud father. "I gave her some tips, of course."

"If he hadn't, it wouldn't look—or taste—half this good," Lilah said. It was true. She glanced with pride at the huge dutch oven filled with big chunks of pork in barbecue sauce, the giant bowls of rice and pinto beans and the basket containing three dozen corn muffins, which might or might not be enough. Without Jesse's advice, that the pork didn't have to be browned for a dish like this, she'd still be browning it.

"Mexican food night," Daniel said. "Perfect time for a serious family council."

Lilah felt uneasy, but the boys leaned forward, chewing happily. They were not at all dreading a "serious family council" but anticipating something interesting. Will dashed to the line of dishes on the kitchen counter to grab another corn muffin, and Daniel waited patiently for him to return.

"It has come to my attention," he said, forking up a bite of pork and rice, "that Jason's sixteenth birthday is next week and Maury's is just two weeks later. That means they'll be eligible for junior driver's licenses."

The younger boys stared at them with awe bordering on worship.

"A license piles a lot of responsibility on the driver's shoulders," Daniel continued.

Lilah listened. In her world, a driver's license had just piled more responsibility on her. It had meant she had to do the grocery shopping, had to pick up her mother and then her father at work, because they only had one rattletrap car, and if she was going to take it to school in the morning, she had to pay the price in the afternoon. Homework had to wait until she'd fulfilled her family duties.

"Not to drink," Jason said.

"Not to pile a bunch of kids into the car and take them places they're not supposed to be," Maury said.

"And to help with some of the errands," Daniel added.

"No problem."

Lilah could tell both boys were trying to hide their excitement. "Buy groceries when we're out of something important. Like popcorn," Jason said, twisting his mouth into a smile that was so like Daniel's it made Lilah smile. Daniel was Jason's superhero, and as far as she could tell, he'd chosen a darned good one.

"Let's see. What else?" Daniel frowned.

"Getting to their jobs on time?"

That came from Jonathan. Lilah stared at him, amazed that he knew more about the dynamic of this family than she did.

Daniel explained, "When they can drive themselves, Jason will be doing odd jobs on Ian's farm every afternoon, and Maury can go to Mike's Diner afternoons and weekends." He paused, and the pause was dramatic. "Which means we have to add two cars. Used cars, naturally, so we're going shopping for trendy junkers on Saturday. All of us," he said, glancing at Lilah and Jesse. "Forget the cleaning. Hamburgers on the grill for dinner. This is a big event. We need everybody's imput."

Lilah could think of worse ways to spend a Saturday than that. She attacked her own dinner at last, allowed herself a second corn muffin slathered with butter and thought about Jonathan. One day, in Daniel's world, he could have a car, too. The rules for being a responsible licensed driver would have been drilled into him from the experiences of Jason and Maury, and she'd be able to relax, knowing everything that could have been done or said had been done or said.

But surely it wasn't possible for life to be that predictable. There had to be a catch somewhere.

## Chapter Six

They stood awestruck in a semicircle around two distinctively different vehicles. Jason gazed, starry-eyed, at a miniscule sports car, its once bright yellow paint dimmed to lemon and scratched in spots, a noticeable dent in its right front fender. The black leather upholstery was cracked with age, and the hood, also black, creaked ominously as the boy tenderly raised it. The car was old, but it would never be a vintage classic.

Maury stood at the rear of a station wagon just like Mike's, but ten years older. Those extra years hadn't been easy, either. He opened the rear hatch, examined the interior and closed it again. He'd done that five or six times while everyone waited for the salesman on the used car lot to finish the paperwork.

"He's figuring the volume and how to pack the food containers," Daniel murmured. "When he's eighteen, he can help Mike haul food to his catering jobs."

He sighed, a sigh of satisfaction. "Well, we did it. Yes," he said to the salesman who'd just joined them, "where do I sign?"

A few minutes later he said, "Jesse, you can ride shotgun with Maury. Lilah," he turned toward her with an imploring look on his face, "would you mind taking Will and Nick and Jonathan home? Because I," he said grandly, "get to ride in the sports car."

"It'll be a treat for me. I've been wanting to spend some time alone with these guys."

The boys raced for her car without a protest and settled themselves into the backseat. Pulling out of the lot, she glanced into the rearview mirror and saw Daniel gazing at her, and the expression on his face startled her. There was warmth in that gaze, but Daniel was always warm. This was something else. Longing? When their eyes connected, she felt a stab of electricity that sizzled through her from head to toe. For a moment she held the contact, looking into the depths of his mysterious milk-chocolate eyes, unable to break the connection. Nor could he. She saw a flash of surprise cross his face, as if the brief spell had startled him as much as it had her.

"Are you okay, Mom?" Jonathan sounded anxious.

She turned her gaze back toward the road, away from Daniel, breathless and quivering inside. "Just great," she said cheerfully. "Let's go home and have ourselves some fun."

"Wow, that was cool," Jonathan said. "I'm going to have a car when I'm sixteen."

"You turn sixteen and you get a car?" Will sounded hopeful.

Lilah didn't feel exactly like herself, so it took some effort to sound normal. "Well, no, it's not quite that easy." She smiled, still seeing the image of Daniel in her mind although they were now blocks away from the car lot. "You also have to learn to drive."

"I hope mine's a Porsche," Jonathan said.

"Dream on," Lilah said. "You'll be thrilled with whatever it is. Hey, when we get home, we should get to work on dinner."

"Daniel says it's warm enough for a picnic," Nick said.

"Yep," Lilah agreed, "and it'll be just like the Fourth of July. Jesse has baked beans in the oven, and we made potato salad last night." She remembered something else she'd been thinking about. "You know, July really is birthday month around here. Jason's, then Maury's, and then Daniel's. Jesse told me."

"Jason told me they have parties on their birthdays," Will said.

"Jesse says Daniel won't let us give him one," Nick said.

Maybe it was just seeing the expression on Daniel's face a few minutes earlier, but Lilah felt like doing something special for him, and the bud of an idea began to blossom.

"Maybe we should give him one anyway," she said slowly. "A surprise party."

THE MINUTE THEY GOT home, the boys began setting up the backyard for a picnic. A black-and-white checked oilcloth tablecover, its edges trimmed with pinking shears, covered the picnic table. From each corner a weight dangled, not a decorative weight, either, but a rock wrapped in cheesecloth and tied on with kitchen twine.

Lilah smiled. Daniel ran a no-frills operation for sure. While the boys were in the house gathering the tableware, she made a bouquet of dark pink peonies cut from the plants that had just begun to bloom at the side of the house. She stood in the yard holding them, frowning. Daniel was getting a proper vase for his birthday, whether he liked it or not. In the meantime…

She found a clear plastic pitcher in a cupboard, and once she'd lined it with huge, bright-green hosta leaves, it looked pretty nice filled with peonies.

She put it down in the center of the table, where the boys were fitting flimsy paper plates into wicker holders. Under each holder and plate was a paper napkin, and on top, a knife and fork from their everyday stainless steel held everything down.

"No plastic forks?"

"Jesse said if we bought plastic forks, we'd probably start washing them and using them again," Nick explained. "So why buy plastic?"

Now everyone was home and everything was under control. Lilah sat on one of the lawn chairs that were arranged around the backyard and relaxed. While Jesse got the fire going in the grill, the younger boys were practicing some soccer moves they'd learned at camp and talking about the events of the day. Jason and Maury were bonding with their new vehicles, simply sitting in them or stroking the hoods, vacuuming the floorboards and exchanging some car talk. Daniel was in the middle of the fray, attempting to act as referee. Unfortunately, Aengus had also joined the impromptu game and was jumping, barking and chasing the ball.

"Hey, Mom, watch this," Jonathan shouted.

Lilah turned and watched her son bounce the ball on top of his sneaker, then toss it in the air and kick it hard. The other boys cheered his move, and Lilah laughed. Her son was flourishing in his new life, thanks to these boys. Her gaze drifted to Daniel. And thanks to this man. Could it be, was it possible, that she was flourishing, too?

She watched as Daniel encouraged the boys, cheering every bounce and kick. Bruce had made her want never to be with a man again, but Daniel was different from any other man she'd known.

He was kind. Patient. Funny. Appealing. Watching him play with the boys, Lilah noticed the graceful way he moved, as if he were comfortable in his own skin.

Her gaze lingered, and a tingle ran through her. Well, of course, it was hard to be a female and not tingle at the sight of him. He was great to look at, but he wasn't just a pretty face. He radiated energy and life, and when he smiled, he could take her breath away.

There was danger here. She could so easily get caught up in that circle of energy and lose what she'd so painfully acquired over the past three years. She could find herself relaxing, staying right here, taking care of his house, mothering his boys, not even realizing she'd lost her independence and had given him control of her life.

He must have sensed her looking at him because suddenly he stopped, and then he sent her that slow smile of his. Lilah felt attraction dance down her spine like a caress, and without thinking, she found herself smiling back.

For a long moment, Daniel simply gazed at her. She wished she knew what was going on in his mind. She hoped he didn't know what she was thinking.

"Aargh!" In pursuit of the ball, Aengus knocked him flat. For a moment, he lay on the summer-green grass, laughing while Aengus frantically licked his face, either apologizing or trying to bring his master back to life.

"Enough, enough," Daniel told the anxious dog. "I'm fine." Still laughing, he rolled up onto his feet, dusted himself off and headed toward Lilah's chair.

"Chow time," Jesse yelled.

"For the record, guys, you may not eat in your cars or sleep in your cars," Daniel megaphoned to Jason and Maury. "That's enough soccer for tonight," he called out to the younger boys. "Come over here and have a hamburger."

A light breeze cooled their picnic. The black flies seemed to have gone to bed, and even though it was still light at seven, citronella candles were lit to discourage the mosquitoes.

"The idea was to have an easy dinner so everybody could go on the field trip to used car lots," he said, spooning up baked beans from the gallon-sized crock. "So what's all this other stuff doing here?" He was sitting beside Lilah, and the twinkling gaze he rested on her made her feel warm inside. A little too warm.

His thigh brushed hers, a firm, muscular thigh, and

the heat inside her intensified. Her appetite, for food, at least, flew away in the evening air.

This was ridiculous. What if the boys noticed her flushed face? She was their housekeeper. She had no business gazing at Daniel with her mouth hanging open.

She closed it tightly, but she couldn't reason the feelings away. "Are you boys going to learn everything you can about engines?" she asked brightly. "So you can do some of your own repairs?"

They were on second and third helpings and having a lively discussion about suspension systems when the candles suddenly flickered and the leaves from the maples rustled. Seconds later, a jagged flash of lightning crackled above them, and to Lilah's amazement, the younger boys immediately began counting. "Seven," they shouted when the thunder rolled.

They gazed at each other and at the sky. "Dessert inside," Jesse said succinctly. "Everybody scramble."

"WE NEED RAIN," Daniel said.

"Not this much of it," Jesse grumbled.

Lightning lit up the picnic scene outside, and thunder rattled the old glass of the windows. They'd barely made it indoors with the food when the heavens opened. Rain pelted down on Jason and Maury while they gathered up soggy paper plates after putting their cars to bed in the carriage house. Maybe even with a good-night kiss.

But Daniel really did need the rain. In the first place, Lilah's fragile body so close to him had stirred his blood, and he didn't want his blood stirred. He was walking a fine line here, having a woman in his house, a beautiful woman, and he didn't dare cross it. He needed the rain to cool him down.

In the second place, he'd been looking for just the right time to explain the foster-care center to her in a casual way. "Before we have shortcake, I have some entertainment planned."

The boys were pitching in, filling trash bags with the used plates, refilling plastic cups from the pitchers of lemonade. "I'll need some tech help in the living room," he added.

"Whoa!" He blocked the kitchen doorway as all five boys attempted to trade kitchen duty for tech assistance. "Jason and Jonathan, come with me."

"Is it a movie?" Nick asked, when he saw the screen set up against the living room windows.

"No, I need to practice the speech I have to give in a couple of weeks to a bunch of people who need to approve the foster-care center. If I wow 'em, they might even donate money."

The boys wriggled uneasily. "Come on," he said. "I help with your homework, right? Well, this is my homework. Pretend you're a roomful of big shots deciding whether to trust me with a great big project I want to do, using their money."

Lilah, who'd been looking interested, winced when he mentioned "other people's money." Bad news. If she wasn't looking forward to the speech, either, he might as well give up on it, he thought, since she was his prime target. He wanted to be able to talk to her about the center. She seemed to understand human nature. She might have some good advice for him.

Jason was at the computer and Jonathan stood by the light switches. First, Daniel delivered a short introduction explaining the purpose of the center.

"The kids would live in houses with parents, just like we live with you?" Maury said. "That's cool."

Jason gave him a look. "Sorry, Daniel," Maury said. "Go on."

The first of the PowerPoint visuals appeared on the screen, presenting a picture of rolling land, grassy and shaded by trees, partially surrounded by a forest of evergreens, maples and birches, with the mountains rising up in the background. Sheep dotted the landscape. "This is the land where we'll build the center. It's…"

"It's Uncle Ian's land," Nick said with an air of authority. "I know from the sheep."

"That's right," Daniel said. "Jason?"

The second image appeared. "This is the architect's model of the center, as you'd see it from the air."

"Like from a helicopter?" Jonathan asked.

"Big shots don't ask that kind of question," Jason informed him.

"Yes," Daniel said, "it's like an aerial view, but these are small models on a tabletop, so the photographer just leaned over them with his camera."

"It looks real," Will said.

An impatient sigh came from Jason, but Daniel said, "Good, because I want the development board to see how it will look."

He hazarded a glance at Lilah. She wasn't wincing now or looking bored—or as if she wished she could go to the kitchen and help Jesse clean up. She was spellbound. Her hair swung over her shoulders as she leaned forward, her eyes sparkling and her cheeks flushed with excitement.

*She* is *beautiful* flashed through his mind, before he thought, *and she's interested.* He was so anxious to hear what she thought about his impending presentation after the boys went to bed that he had to force himself not to rush through the rest of his speech and to be patient when the boys interrupted him with questions. The slides got pretty boring anyway toward the end— not for him but for his restless audience, which became increasingly fidgety as the smell of baking shortcake wafted in from the kitchen.

Lilah didn't look bored, not even by these slides. When the estimated costs came up on the screen, her forehead wrinkled in concentration. In reaction to the list of potential donors, he could almost see ideas buzzing in her head.

"Any questions?" he asked, when he wound up.

"No," Will said forcefully, gazing toward the kitchen.

"No questions?" He gave them his most disappointed face, then his hopeful one. "Does this mean you're ready to donate?"

"I'll give you all the allowance I've saved, if you'll just let us have that strawberry shortcake," Will said fervently.

Daniel looked severely around the room. "Anybody else?"

"Dessert's ready," Jesse bellowed from the kitchen.

"Good night, then," Daniel said, bowing. "I'll be in touch with you soon, and have your checkbooks with you."

He said it to an audience of one—Lilah, who was still gazing at the final slide showing the projected time frame for building the center.

A brilliant flash of lightning and a deafening clap of thunder punctuated the moment. *Gotcha,* Daniel thought.

ONCE AGAIN, BEDTIME DIDN'T happen exactly at nine, but at last the boys and Jesse were, if not exactly quiet, at least tucked away behind closed doors. Lilah was so wrapped up in the center proposal that she realized she'd done a pretty poor job of seeing the kids off to bed.

"I could stand another cup of coffee," Daniel said. "How about you?"

She heard him, but couldn't concentrate on anything as trivial as coffee. "Wow," she said softly, "what you're doing here is, well, it's just…just the most wonderful thing imaginable. And you have it so well thought out. You must have been planning it for years."

He paused at the door, walked back toward her and sat across from her. "You think I'm on the right track?" he said. "You think I can convince the Regional Development Board it's a good idea? Because without them, I can't get the permits to build, and without those, there's no point in fund-raising."

"Of course you'll convince them…" Her voice trailed off.

"But?" he said. "You have to tell me. That's what this trial run was all about."

"I was thinking…"

"What were you thinking."

Okay, she'd go for it.

"I was thinking about some ways you could jazz up the presentation."

His eyebrows lifted. "Tell me. I need to bowl these folks over."

"Well, entertaining them would be a good start. What about a film with a voice-over." She warmed to her subject. "What about a panoramic view of the property, which is beautiful, by the way, then a…well, almost a realistic tour of the architect's models." She paused for a moment, thinking. "Are there other centers like these?"

"Several," he said. He seemed mesmerized. It gave her courage.

"Maybe someone could do some filming at one of them, show the children engaging in activities there, a clip of the kids having dinner at one of the houses—I thought of that because dinner is such fun here, a high point in the boys' days. No close-ups of their faces, of course," she added in a hurry, "for obvious reasons, but maybe a clip of them in their recreation center, and on their playing fields, and maybe even one of them piling into the bus that takes them to school every day."

She'd been letting her gaze wander as ideas spilled out, but now she focused on him and found him staring back at her.

"It's my turn to say, 'Wow,'" he said after a long pause. He began to pace. "You are so right."

A thrill ran through her. He'd listened to her, and he liked what he'd heard. It made her feel more worthwhile than she'd felt in years.

He went on, "There's a guy in the valley who could do it, Ray Colloton, lives in LaRocque. I think he'd give us a good price. We could fly him to one of the centers...."

He stopped pacing and sat down, looking her straight in the eyes. "Maybe you could go with him and show him what we want."

"Oh, I couldn't," she said. "I have a job to do here."

"I," Daniel said, pointing in the direction of the clinic, "have a job to do there."

"I know how busy you are. I have no idea how you can keep up your practice and give this project what it needs. The details, the endless details, are simply staggering."

His gaze hadn't wavered. "Think you could handle a few of them for me?"

## Chapter Seven

Lilah stared at him. "I'd like that coffee now," she said.

At least she hadn't said no or argued that she already had enough to do. "Coming right up," Daniel said, "so don't go away."

He got the coffee started, then thought he'd better wait for it with Lilah in his line of sight so she couldn't escape. He went back to the living room, and there he found her gazing at a blank wall. "Hello?" he said. "Are you still with us here on earth?"

She shot him a smile and seemed to relax. "To answer your question, of course I'm happy to help in any way I can. The house is running smoothly, and I have time to think about the center, too."

"You wouldn't feel imposed upon?"

"Of course not. I'm full-time. I'll use that time however you want me to." A shadow crossed her face. "Is the coffee just about ready?" she asked, sounding as if she really needed it.

As always, he had no idea what he might have said to cause her sudden look of doubt. "I imagine so." The coffee wasn't, quite, so he waited and watched it drip while he pondered her contradictions, her happiness, her unexpected moments of...of what? Worry? Sadness? Was she grieving for her husband?

The muscles of his back knotted. How did that scar on her forehead fit into the picture?

He relaxed a bit and laughed at himself. His knee-jerk reaction to protect the young and the helpless had probably made him imagine the scar was a result of abuse. She'd probably fallen on the ice or been thrown by a horse. And of course she'd be grieving for her husband.

He'd felt her response to him, though, the few times he'd accidentally touched her. The truth was, he'd like to touch her on purpose. What he wanted... He suddenly knew what he wanted, and it unnerved him. He wanted to take her in his arms, hug her tight and kiss her. The way her full pink lips had opened as she gazed so raptly at his presentation—maybe even at him—had opened up something in him he'd wanted to keep closed.

But she was his employee. He'd practically coerced her into taking this job, and to make a sexual approach to her would violate every principle of an honorable employer/employee relationship. Not only that, but an affair wasn't what he wanted at this point in his life. He was pretty happy. His life was stable.

Someday, maybe, he'd be ready for love of the romantic kind, but he could never "take a chance on love." He had to have certainty. He'd have to trust the woman completely. Rejection, betrayal, could destroy him.

He had no clue as to what went on inside Lilah or what her life story was, what had driven such a valuable woman into the situation in which he'd found her. Until he learned the answers to those questions, there was no certainty, and he needed those things more than he needed love—or even sex.

He sighed. His libido, so long suppressed, had inexplicably sabotaged his good judgment. What he really wanted was simply to have her working for him.

That was his story and he was sticking to it.

The coffeepot seemed to take forever. He focused on the bouquet in the middle of the kitchen table—his Siberian Irises had just started blooming and Lilah had stuck some of them in here and there with more of the snowball heads. It looked pretty, even on the same old tablecloth. That hadn't changed. Even she knew cloth covers would be a laundry disaster.

Maybe he'd just confused flowers and a neat living room with stability.

When at last the coffee seemed to be ready, he spilled it all over the counter, because he was trying to pour it as fast as he could. One more minute of worry that he was getting too close to her might have led to heart failure. Arrhythmia, anyway. He had to keep her at arm's length—literally.

Before he could carry the cups into the living room, Lilah appeared in the kitchen with a sheaf of copy paper in her hand and a look of intense concentration on her face. "The slides of the financial stuff aren't exactly gripping," she said, sitting down at the kitchen table, "so I was thinking zippier graphics might perk them up.

Catchy fonts, larger, too, lots of color, bullets and arrows. Here. Look at this. It's just a rough plan of how the pages might be laid out."

He put the coffee on the table and sat, amused by her seriousness but feeling his senses tingle, coming back to life after years of numbness. She handed him several sheets of paper.

"You could put the same material in a handout that they could take home with them."

He grinned at her. "Maybe we should skip the housekeeping and hire you as public relations officer for the center."

"Oh, no, these are just some ideas…"

He felt confident enough to tease her. "Think about it. We'd send out a press release, "Lilah Jamison has accepted the position of…""

"No press release." She snapped it at him. "No newspapers." She must have seen how she'd startled him, because her mouth twisted in a rueful smile. "Sorry. I overreacted. I'm just averse to publicity, always have been." She sighed. "My mother always said your name should never be in the newspaper except at birth and death. I guess it sank in."

He gazed at her, then relaxed, just as she had done, and said, "She must have been a real lady. Tell me about her."

He saw her tense up again. "Oh, she's just a mom," she said lightly. "A working mom. My dad's an auto mechanic. We were poor but happy, as the saying goes."

She'd obviously ended that conversational thread. He gave up—for the moment—on trying to glean a scrap of personal information from her. "Okay, let's look at those sketches of yours. Do you do computer graphics?"

She gazed at him, and it was as if a veil dropped over her face, and when she spoke, she sounded bitter. "I do very compelling computer graphics."

Lilah had a secret. Until he knew the secret, he wouldn't know her, and he couldn't trust her completely. With the boys, yes, but not with his heart.

LILAH SAID GOOD-NIGHT TO Daniel as soon as she could. When she reached her apartment, she fell across the bed and buried her face in the pillows.

She had done the fliers for Bruce's nonexistent housing development. She'd learned to keep his books, and then she'd had to learn how to do computer graphics. She'd found it fun, much more fun than spreadsheets. He'd handed her blueprints and sketches of finished houses, and she'd scanned, reduced, enlarged and cropped to make the envelope of promotional material as appealing to potential purchasers as possible. She didn't know he'd simply bought the blueprints from a home-building magazine.

She'd had no idea she was facilitating his scam, but still she felt guilty for making such a good case for North Woods, the development that would never be built.

What had shaken her this evening was the memory of Bruce commanding her to learn how to do the graphics and produce the materials. He'd said, "I support you, so you'll damned well do what I want you to do with your time."

What she'd said to Daniel was, "I'm full-time, so I'll

do whatever you want me to do with that time." Which meant the same thing. And when she'd heard the words spilling out of her mouth, she'd felt sick.

But Daniel wasn't like Bruce. He hadn't commanded her, he'd asked her. The center must be real, although she'd had a moment of worry as he talked about asking for donations to build it.

She needed to put her life with Bruce behind her. And she'd thought she had—until she found herself in close contact with a man who could just as easily rob her of her independence, even though he'd do it nicely, make her think dependence was just what she wanted.

But she couldn't spend her life looking for similarities to Bruce in every man she met. She had to get over it.

AT BREAKFAST THE NEXT morning, Jason and Maury slipped envelopes into Daniel's hand. Surprised by the gesture, he found an excuse to leave the room in order to see what was inside.

The note from Maury read,

Dear Daniel: Thank you so much for my car. I promise to be careful driving it. I'll keep it clean and try to get the best gas mileage I can. I can't wait until my birthday when I can drive it by myself, but I like it when you're in the front seat, Jesse and Lilah, too. So anytime you want to ride with me is fine. Your friend, Maury.

Daniel smiled. He was touched by Maury's note. He was a great kid. Maybe he'd never be a great poet, but he didn't need to be because he'd be a great cook.

Next, he opened Jason's letter.

Dear Daniel: I want to say some things I can't say to your face. You changed my life. When I came here, I was so mad I wanted to make things as hard for everyone around me as I could. Now I can't even remember how it felt to be that mad. You made me know I could trust you. You acted like you liked me, so I started to think maybe other people could like me, too. I found out they do, and everything in my life feels different.

When you gave Maury and me these cars, it meant you trusted me. I don't ever want to let you down. You are too good a man for anybody to let you down. Thank you for the car, for making me feel this way, and for being the greatest person I've ever known. Jason.

Daniel read the note, then read it again. His eyes stung. This might be his finest moment. Building the foster-care center would pale in comparison.

When he felt in control, he went back to the kitchen, where the boys were talking about Harry Potter's latest adventure over stacks of French toast. Jason and Maury were sitting side by side, and he paused between them, ruffling their hair. "Thanks," he whispered.

It was enough. Maury blushed, and Jason looked up at him. Daniel tried to transmit, without words, the message, *You're special to me. I love you as if you were my own sons.*

He saw Lilah across the table, taking in the scene, her facial expression ever-changing, as if she were wondering how the boys' notes had affected him. He had no doubt that writing the notes had been her idea, but the words had come straight from the boys' hearts.

And had gone straight to his.

"I THINK WE'VE GOT Jason's party together," Jesse said. "I'm off to take a shower before he and Daniel get home."

"Good plan," Lilah said. "I'll make a cup of tea and keep an eye on the scalloped potatoes."

"Call me if they get home with good news," Jesse said as he limped out of the room. "I'll come out stark naked to congratulate Jason if I have to."

"I'd love it if you didn't," Lilah said.

She went to the window and rested her forehead against the cool glass. This was such a big day for Jason. His sixteenth birthday, and he would get his Junior Operator's License if he passed the test. They were blowing it all out for his party, and he'd invited five friends, four of them kids who were in and out of the house all the time and wouldn't run screaming from the noise and general confusion. Lilah had her fingers crossed for the fifth one. She smiled. He'd pass the test. His party would be a victory celebration.

"Mom?"

She whirled. "Jonathan! You scared me. I guess I was daydreaming. How're you doing, sweetie? Pretty big day, huh?"

"Yeah. Mom, where do you think Dad is?"

She led him to the kitchen table and sat down across from him. "I don't know," she said, wanting to be honest. "I know he's out of prison, and I know he told a reporter he wanted to be with us again, but that's all."

"Do you want to be with him again?"

What had brought on his anxiety? "No," she said. Then, dreading the answer, she asked, "Do you miss him?"

"Uh-uh. No way."

His head was downcast, and his sneakers kicked the chair stretchers. "Honey, what's worrying you?"

He answered with another question. "Are you happy here?"

"Why, yes," she said, realizing it was true. "And you are, too, I think."

He raised his head and his face brightened. "Oh, yeah. I have kids to play with all the time, and everybody's nice, and you're right here when I need you."

"So what's the problem?" She smiled at him.

"I'm scared he'll find us, and we'll have to run away again."

Her smile faded. She leaned back in the chair, then was suddenly filled with resolve. "Maybe we won't run away anymore, Jonathan. Maybe we're ready to stand up for ourselves."

"They're home!" Will shrieked. His yell rattled the windows. Jonathan was up and running, his worry temporarily forgotten in the excitement of finding out if Jason had passed the test. Looking out the window again, seeing Daniel standing beside Jason, who seemed even taller now, both of them trying to look casual and failing to, she knew it was a victorious homecoming.

Her gaze went to Daniel and lingered there. He wore chinos with a white polo shirt. She smiled. She'd already washed that shirt half a dozen times. It must be a favorite of his. Or maybe it was just the shirt on top of the stack.

Even this early in the summer, his arms were browned by the sun, his nose sunburned. His sun-streaked hair was windblown from the ride in the sports car. He started toward the house and Lilah watched his easy, ambling gait, graceful and confident, never hurried. Nick and Jonathan clung to him, and as she watched, he captured each one in the crook of an arm, picked them up and swung them around in the air.

He was an amazing man. She wished…

She sighed. If wishes were horses…

She bolted through the kitchen door and headed for the celebration, wanting to be a part of it as much as Jonathan did.

Or did she just want to be closer to Daniel.

"AS SOON AS JASON'S friends get here we're ready," Lilah said, wiping her hands on her apron—Jesse's apron, actually.

"They'd better hurry," Jesse groused. "Will's gonna eat the dog if they don't turn up soon."

"A car's pulling into the drive right now," Daniel said from the hallway. "I'll call Jason."

"He's already outside," Jesse said.

Daniel joined Lilah at the window, watching four kids spill out of a van belonging to Ray Waller, Jeff's dad. "I thought Jason said five friends. I only see four."

"Somebody got sick, I imagine," Lilah said. "What a shame."

"Or lives close enough to walk." Daniel watched as Jason reached the car and saw him engage in serious conversation with Jeff and his dad. "Looks like 'sick and can't come,'" he said. "Jason looks too serious for a birthday boy."

"I'll keep an eye on him," Lilah said.

An image butterflied through Daniel's mind, of Lilah hugging Jason when they got home, and Jason letting her.

And then he saw another image. When the whole crew had come back, he'd caught her eye, and the impact of that look of shared emotion—*Jason's happy, you're happy, and that makes me happy*—had made his pulse race.

But, then, it had been an emotional day.

The avalanche hit the kitchen, Daniel's boys, Jason's friends, and Aengus in the midst of them. The party had begun.

"DOWN!" DANIEL SPED TOWARD the kitchen counter where the cake was on display, and moved Aengus's paws from directly in front of it. "Dogs eat steak, not cake," he told his pet.

The dog had the good grace to look faintly ashamed before he loped away in search of dinner leftovers on the picnic tables outside.

Daniel took a close look at the cake. A yellow sports car, and a darned good replica of one, too, except that it sat a lot lower and looked a lot longer than Jason's car, because you needed a lot of cake to feed this bunch. Lilah had artistic skills, that was for sure. And the way the presentation visuals were shaping up was...

"Daniel."

He jumped. Lilah had sneaked up behind him, and the breathy way she said his name made him shiver. Instead of turning, afraid of what she might see on his face, he continued to gaze at the cake.

"I'm afraid you're right. Everybody's having a great time except Jason."

He turned to face her. "Because of the guest who couldn't come, you think? Maybe a girl he's interested in stood him up." He sighed. "I'll talk to him."

"HER FATHER WOULDN'T LET her come."

Jason had come to him. Daniel hadn't had to corner him to find out why Melissa hadn't come to the party. That was the only positive note in the situation. Jason's shoulders drooped, and his face was downcast. Aengus put his head on Jason's knee and he rubbed the dog behind the ears.

"Why?" Daniel asked him. "She's too young? Not allowed to date yet?"

Jason stood up, angry now instead of dejected. "Not allowed to go out with me. Her father won't let her go out with anybody unless he knows the family."

"I'm your family," Daniel said, unable to control the tensing of the muscles in his face.

"Try telling him that. Jeff's dad tried when they went to pick her up. He was really mad when he got back to the car."

A range of feelings shot through Daniel, empathy for Jason, and the feeling he feared most, absolute, consuming fury at a man who mistrusted a boy just because he was in a foster home. It was the only reason the man could have had. Jason was an excellent student, skillful at basketball and soccer. Whoever this father was, he should be proud Jason had shown an interest in his daughter.

He had to hide his rage from the boy, keep his voice down and his fists from clenching. "What's Melissa's last name?"

"Wilcox."

Daniel sighed. "Oh, boy. That is really too bad."

Jason's eyes asked a question.

"Ed Wilcox is a dairy farmer. He's one of the most vocal opponents of the foster-care center, so he's not too fond of me. Besides that, he's a skinflint, never gives to any cause, doesn't even take proper care of his cows. He's negative about everything, Jason. It's not you, it's just the way Ed is."

"But he's Melissa's father, and she's the nicest girl in the whole school," Jason protested.

"It happens sometimes," Daniel said.

"It wasn't her fault it happened." A suspicious moisture glazed Jason's eyes, and his body drooped. "She'd already asked her mother, her mother said yes, then her father wanted to know who she was going out with and freaked. She feels really bad. She says we can still see each other at school. She's not the kind of girl who'd sneak off on a date."

"Which is one of the reasons you like her. I'm so

sorry, Jason," Daniel said. "I could have a talk with Ed, but I don't want to make things worse."

"They couldn't be any worse." Suddenly Jason straightened his shoulders and rose. "It was a great party, Daniel. Aengus and I are going up to bed. I'll talk it over with Maury."

He paused at the door. "You can tell Lilah and Jesse," he said. "I don't want them to think I didn't like the party."

Daniel joined him in the doorway and put his hand on Jason's shoulder. "You're a fine person, Jason. Don't let one man make you think you're not."

"Thanks." Jason gave him a crooked smile. "Lilah makes a heck of a car cake, doesn't she?"

Lilah was a heck of a woman. Maybe she could help him decide what to do about Ed Wilcox.

# Chapter Eight

"That horrible man," Lilah said. Her eyes flashed dangerously. "He's closed-minded, disrespectful of his daughter's judgment…"

"And bad to his cows," Daniel said gloomily.

The flashing eyes landed on him. "From anybody else, I'd think that was a joke," she said.

"Well, not from me. He's a bad man all around."

"He must have some good in him," she protested. "Everybody does."

"You find it. I can't. He's as stingy with his goodwill toward man as he is with his money."

"All right, I will." She simmered for a few minutes.

"He's dead set against the center, for the same reasons he's dead set against Jason dating his daughter. He and Virginia Galloway are our most formidable opponents, I think. Virginia can influence churchwomen all over the valley, and Ed, believe it or not, has somehow established himself in the Dairy Farmers' Association."

"You'll just have to win them over," she announced.

"How the heck am I supposed to do that?"

"I don't even know them. Let's think about it."

She'd come into the living room brandishing her latest drafts of visuals for the meeting, and for the first time she'd sat down beside him on the sofa so they could look at them together. That meant he was close to that slim, serious face, with the frown she always had when she was thinking. It helped his anger fade.

He drummed his fingers on the arm of the sofa. "The only way I can think of to win Ed over is to give him a whole bunch of money."

"That would be bribery," she said primly.

"As for Virginia, hmm, something to run. Something to star in."

She snapped her fingers. "Give them important volunteer jobs for the center."

"Huh?" He was flabbergasted. Last thing he wanted was to have Virginia and Ed messing with his center.

"Yes, volunteer jobs. If they get involved, well, you know what they say in politics."

"No, I don't know what they say in politics," Daniel said, wondering where the conversation was drifting.

"A volunteer is a vote."

He contemplated the concept. "That makes sense."

"What job could Virginia do that would make her feel important?"

"I don't know. Take over the whole project?"

She gave him a look. "Be serious. What sorts of jobs need to be done right now?"

He began to list them, and after he said, "We'll be asking for grants, and the grant proposals will require projected capital expense and operating expense reports. You know, the cleaning, maintenance, food, equipment of various sorts..." he trailed off.

"What?" Lilah said. "What did you just think of?"

"Well," he said slowly, "Virginia used to be a nutritionist. Maybe she'd be willing to plan a month of menus, estimate the cost."

"That's a great idea! She can form a committee. She'd be the chairman, of course, and she could command her minions to do the pricing and then have total control over the menus."

"Okay," he said, still feeling doubtful. "I'll give it a try. Any ideas for Ed? Volunteer strangler?"

"Money," she said thoughtfully. "Virginia would be pricing food without actually buying it, so what could Ed do that would make him *feel* as if he were spending a lot of money?"

"Sports equipment," Daniel breathed. "He was a star football player in high school." He wagged a warning finger. "Don't ever ask him about it unless you have an hour or two to listen to him say, 'And then there was that win against Brattleboro High...' Anyway, he could figure out what we'll need and check all over the state to price the equipment."

"Good," Lilah said. "That problem's solved. Now could I show you these charts?"

"I'm at your service."

To look at the charts, he had to lean closer to her, look over her shoulder. Her hair, which looked shinier and healthier every day, tickled his cheek. He began thinking really dumb thoughts. For example, imagining that she was his dreamcatcher, sent by fate to banish his nightmares. And that she'd flown into his life unexpectedly to inspire him to achieve greater things. And worse, he was realizing how much he didn't want her to fly away.

She was so close, just a kiss away. Her generous mouth shone, blinding his common sense. He moved a millimeter nearer, or maybe it was only his heart that moved.

"We'll look at these visuals tomorrow," she said, leaping up with all her papers clutched tight in her hands. "Virginia and Ed were a much more important issue."

She gave him a bright smile and did what he was afraid she'd do—she flew.

IF YOU RUN FAST ENOUGH, the monster won't catch you. In the safety of the carriage house she laid out her drafts on the coffee table and tried to regain her earlier excitement, to no avail. All she could see was Daniel's face so close to hers, hinting at a kiss that would have been so easy, so natural, so wonderful—a moment that might be gone forever.

Would she regret it? At the moment, yes. She sighed, rearranged the papers in a neat stack and went to bed, wondering what it would be like to be kissed by Daniel. She had a strong and scary feeling that it would be absolutely blissful.

THE TWO WEEKS LILAH and Jonathan had lived in their car had seemed like an eternity, but the following two weeks hurtled by with the speed and force of a tidal wave.

The Fourth of July came and went with the proverbial bang. Fireworks, a parade in town, barbecued chicken that the Rotary Club members had gotten up at four in the morning to have ready by noon, and a great picnic in the backyard in the evening.

Lilah had paid a visit to the photographer Daniel had suggested. "Don't let him scare you," Daniel had warned her. "His skills are camera skills, not social skills."

She was glad he'd prepared her. Ray Colloton was a dour man with a growly voice that he used as little as possible. She struggled valiantly through her spiel, to which he appeared not to have the slightest reaction, so she was shocked when she finally stopped talking and he said without even a ghost of a smile, "Sure. I'll donate my time and materials. You pay travel expenses."

"Free!" She was so excited she tackled Daniel right outside the clinic door on his way into the house. "All Ray wants is travel expenses."

"Nothing like smart, informed female charm," Daniel said.

"It wasn't me, it was the center. You have a fan." But his smile shone above her more brightly than the late-setting sun.

For Maury's birthday, Mike closed the restaurant on Sunday evening—an unprecedented event—and produced a gourmet multi-course dinner, whose various dishes the younger boys either devoured enthusiastically or passed on surreptitiously to Lilah for covert disposal. It ended, whimsically and sentimentally, with the traditional birthday cake and homemade ice cream. Maury's cake, of course, was decorated to resemble a chef wearing a tall white hat.

Maury beamed all evening. Lilah wasn't sure whether it was the reaction to the excitement of the party or the presence of a very pretty girl he pretended not to be gazing at—or the fact that now he could work at the restaurant every afternoon, evening and weekend.

The diner was crammed full. The rest of Daniel's kids were there, of course, plus Maury's school friends. Mike was conspicuous because he was in charge, and Ian was there, too. Mike seemed to be warming to her. Even Ian's glower seemed less fierce.

If only Jason's party could have been so uncomplicated. The winning-over of Ed Wilcox and Virginia Galloway still hung oppressively in the air. Lilah had discovered that summer was Daniel's busiest season, with cows to attend to, horses, pigs, Ian's sheep, tiny Chihuahuas and big huskies, Labs, golden retrievers and Burmese mountain dogs—they seemed to need more attention in the summertime.

Just like kids. As long as you could keep them penned up, they were safe. Let them loose, however, and there was no end to the trouble they could get into.

"Virginia," she reminded Daniel. "Ed. You have to buck up and go for it before the presentation."

"Nag, nag, nag," he said.

She gave him a look. "If you'd already done it, I wouldn't have to nag. And here's some more nagging. We have to schedule the filming. The meeting's two weeks from Tuesday. Ray needs time to edit and splice, to choose background music, all that stuff. You're the one who should go with him," she insisted. "So don't argue with me."

"When you have him in the palm of your hand? When I have more piglets coming, cows with unacceptable cream levels and Bob Frost with an acid reflux reaction to cheesecake? Oh, yes, and there's the fungus between Banjo Galloway's toenails. How he got a fungus is a mystery to me. I don't think Virginia lets him run loose…" He paused, gazing at her face, obviously realizing he'd sealed his own fate.

"When," she asked pointedly, "is Banjo's appointment?"

"Okay, okay."

She could see his exhaustion in the dark circles under his eyes. "Let's make a deal," she suggested. "I'll go with Ray, and you'll pounce on Virginia and Ed."

He threw up his hands in surrender. "Deal. If I can just figure out a way to get to Ed."

"You will," she said, flashing him a smile.

A few days later, the trip with Ray to a foster-care center in Connecticut, celebrated as a model for all future centers, had been interesting. Unique, even. It had meant a long drive with Ray instead of a short flight, which had meant a long interval of silence instead of a short one.

Amazingly, the end result, produced a week later, was a compelling film. Lilah thought about inviting him to dinner with Daniel, Jesse and five energetic boys, and decided that might drive Ray into a deep depression, so instead she made a batch of peanut-butter cookies and hand-delivered them.

With the film behind her, the visuals under control and a week still left before the presentation, she turned her attention to the project that was almost as dear to her heart as the center was to Daniel's.

"VIRGINIA!" DANIEL BEAMED as she swept regally into his examination room with Banjo in her arms. He took the dog from her tenderly, already checking out his toenails. "Looking good," he said. "The ointment's working."

With his hands on Banjo and his eyes on Virginia, he said, "I have a big favor to ask of you. This grant money we're going after for the center…"

Fifteen minutes later Virginia agreed to take charge of the nutritional component of the center's proposal for funding.

He'd spent sleepless nights deciding how to approach Ed, but now Daniel thought he had it aced, so he took a deep breath and dialed Ed's number. The first minute or two of the conversation were uncomfortable, what with Daniel at one end trying to pretend he didn't know Ed had refused to let his daughter come to Jason's party and Ed at the other end obviously wondering if Daniel knew. But at last he got to the clincher.

"Ed, a salesman has dropped off samples of a food supplement for milk cows, and he wants me to test them. If you're agreeable, I'd like to try them out on your cows."

He could almost hear Ed's brain working. *Free food supplements, and the doctor does the driving! What veterinary services can I hit him up for while he's out here asking me for a favor?*

Then there was the trip to Ed's farm with the supplements, which Daniel had actually bought with his
own money. And finally it was Ed wondering if he
wanted to go to the trouble of giving the cows the
supplements.

But he couldn't resist getting something for free.
Daniel took a look at a couple of the cows—no
charge—and then wangled a glass of water. In the main
room of the farmhouse he found the football trophies
that Mike had told him would be there, which Mike had
found out by quizzing his customers.

"Ed, I just realized that since you're a legendary
football star, you're just the guy I need."

It took fifteen minutes more to make sure Ed understood it was a volunteer job.

And then Ed set himself up for the kill. "Talking to
dealers all over the state's going to take a lot of gas."
Ed sent him a shifty look.

"It will," Daniel said, "but not necessarily yours."
Ed's eyes brightened. "I'm assigning you an assistant.
He'll drive you around. Great guy. Tell you what. I'll
treat you both to breakfast at Mike's Diner on Tuesday
morning."

Sold. Ed was already thinking, "Free breakfast!"
Daniel gleefully looked forward to the moment he could
say, "Ed Wilcox, Jason Reeves."

"WAR COUNCIL," LILAH SAID to the boys one day when
Daniel mentioned he'd be late for lunch. "We're going
to give Daniel a birthday party."

"I'm not sure he'll like that," Jason said, frowning.

"Jesse always makes him a cake, and he sort of, you know…"

"Huffs and puffs," Maury said.

"Men are like that when they grow up," Lilah said. "Never want you to make a fuss over them. But I'm not sure that's how they feel inside. So we're going to be brave and find out."

"What do we have to do?" Nick said.

"Not tell him is the first thing," Lilah said. "It'll be a surprise party so he can't do anything to stop it until it's too late. Then we have to get Ian and Mike to co-operate."

"They'll sure do that." Jesse grinned evilly. "They get a kick out of embarrassing each other."

"How can we keep him from finding out?" Nick asked.

Nick of all people, so skilled at keeping secrets.

"We can do the cooking while he's working and stash it in Lilah's refrigerator," Maury said, "and when that gets full, we'll use one of the diner's fridges."

"Yeah," Will said, "and he can walk in for breakfast and see Jesse making the cake, just like last year, and he can do his…"

"Huffing and puffing," Lilah said. She smiled. "Then how can we keep him out late, so we can put it all together?"

"Uncle Ian," Nick said. "He can have a sick sheep. Maybe he'll have a sick sheep for real, but I hope not."

"Maybe just a vitamin deficiency," Jason suggested.

"Whatever," Nick said, "and then they'll talk, and after that Daniel will come home and we'll yell, 'Surprise!' and then Uncle Ian will drive up."

"That'll work," Lilah said. "Uh-oh, I hear the clinic door opening. Everybody scatter."

They scattered straight into Daniel. "What's going on?" he said.

"Lilah was checking our summer reading lists," Jason said.

"And I have to finish *Treasure Island* fast, so I won't get behind schedule," Will said.

When he stepped into the kitchen, Daniel's expression was puzzled, to say the least.

DANIEL WENT OUT THE kitchen door in search of Jason and found him washing his car. Cleanest car in the valley, except for Maury's, which was practically sterilized.

Daniel had made a commitment to Ed without first consulting Jason, and he'd been worrying about it. He wasn't sure he could convince Jason the plan would work.

The plan being that Jason could charm cranky Ed into recognizing him as an acceptable human being. Maybe it wouldn't work. Daniel had no idea how Ed would react, and he had no idea how Jason would react. Ed was the last person on earth Jason wanted to see, talk to, or, worst of all, drive around the state.

But life had taught Daniel that if you had a problem, you had to face it and deal with it. This conversation required considerable tact and diplomacy, so he began by picking up a brush and starting to scrub the fenders. "Still like the car?"

"You're kidding, right?" Jason turned to look at Daniel and grinned. It must have been something in

Daniel's face that made the grin fade. "Is this about Melissa?"

"You're way too intuitive for your own good," Daniel growled, at the same time reminding himself he was trying to get that grin back on Jason's face. "But yes. I wondered how you were doing."

Jason went back to washing the car. "Better. We talked a while at soccer camp. She still likes me. It's just her dad."

Daniel picked up a sponge and started on the hood of the car. "Ed can be difficult."

"He's a jerk."

"Yep," Daniel agreed. "But have you ever heard the expression, 'You catch more flies with honey than with vinegar?'"

"Of course you can. What's that got to do with Mr. Wilcox? He's pure vinegar. Never caught a fly in his life."

"Ed is the fly," Daniel explained. "You're the one with the jar of honey." He shifted to the side of the car. "I got to thinking that if you want to change Ed's mind about you, you need to sneak up on him and show him what a great kid you are. Acting mad won't get you anywhere. But getting him to decide he might have been wrong about you will."

Jason stopped scrubbing. "How?"

"Let me tell you about my afternoon with Ed. He's even more dead set against the center than he is about you, so I…"

He told Jason the whole story, doing impressions of Ed that got Jason laughing so hard he was snorting, and then said, "so I told him you'd be his driver."

Jason dropped the sponge. He looked as if he'd swallowed a worm, a live one. "I'd have to sit in the car, *my* car, with him? Talk to him? No way."

"I'll buy the gas," Daniel said, hoping to get him laughing again. It didn't work.

"I can't do it. What about Uncle Ian? He's expecting me to work on the barn roof."

"Ian will understand. I know it sounds grim," Daniel admitted, "but it seems to me this is the best way to get to him. He'll be able to see for himself that you're good enough for his daughter. Heck," he added, "he may figure it out when the three of us have breakfast at Mike's Tuesday morning."

"Daniel!"

"All you have to do is be calm and polite and tell Ed how much you're looking forward to working with him. Don't mention Melissa. Don't mention the party. Just mention how awesome it is that he has volunteered. A sports hero like him will know all about sports equipment. And don't look at him the way you're looking at me right now, either." He smiled at Jason's dark expression as he explained. "Look earnest." He demonstrated looking "earnest."

"Think of it this way, Jason. It's a game, and it's one you're sure to win. Think of it as getting the best of Ed." He looked Jason directly in the eyes. "And I know it will work, because if I had a daughter, I'd be in hog heaven if she snagged you for her boyfriend."

Jason broke eye contact and didn't say anything for a few minutes. Finally he reached out and took the hose away from Daniel. "Okay, I'll give it a shot," he said, "but I'm not looking forward to it."

"MR. WILCOX," JASON SAID, looking extremely earnest, "it's great you're doing this. Being a football star and all, you must know all about the equipment the center will need." He gave Ed an easy grin. "And I just got a car, so there's nothing I like better than driving it. This'll be fun. Well, thanks for breakfast, Daniel. I'd better head out to soccer camp." He held out his hand to Ed. "Great to meet you, Mr. Wilcox."

Daniel said goodbye and waited, his heart in his throat.

"Seems like a nice enough kid," Ed muttered. "Ay-uh, he'll be okay. Miss!" He summoned the waitress. "Have anything like a cinnamon roll or a…"

Bingo.

EACH WEDNESDAY WHEN THE Northeast Kingdom's paper came out, Lilah scanned the news online. There had been no further mention of Bruce. This could be a good sign or a bad one. He must be working somewhere. She assumed he'd been left as penniless as she was, but maybe not. For all she knew, he'd stashed away money in a Swiss—or Cayman Islands—bank account.

She went on to the News from Whittaker column. "Eleanor McDougal was admitted to the hospital on…"

Mrs. McDougal had been her home care patient these past three years. Lilah had loved her. At ninety-four, comatose and fading away, this might be her last trip to the hospital. Lilah wanted to do something for her—a note to her son?

No, a note would have a postmark, and Mrs. McDougal's son, at least, would know where she was.

Yes, Lilah was being paranoid, but if she made a mistake, she'd pay the price of Bruce's finding her and Jonathan.

Flowers. If she went to a florist here, paid cash and didn't put her name on the card, maybe she could get away with it.

"I have a quick errand to run," she told Jesse. "I need...colored pencils."

"Would you pick up a couple of pounds of butter while you're out? And ten pounds of flour? Oh, yeah, I'd feel better if we had a backup jar of mustard. I'm using the last one. And, let's see..."

Lilah sighed, got out her notebook and made a list.

At the Rose Red florist shop, she selected the types of flowers she wanted in the arrangement—flowers that were blooming now in Vermont. Lush pink peonies, deep-purple irises, accented with delicate white sprigs of lily-of-the-valley. "The florist in Whittaker will have these flowers," the Churchill florist said. "It will be a beautiful gift."

"It will have the Whittaker florist's name on it, won't it?" Lilah was still feeling nervous about what she was doing.

"Yes," Melinda said, looking miffed. "Even though I was the one who helped you design it. What message for the card?"

"'Please feel better,'" Lilah told her. "'I miss you.' And that's it."

"Got it. It will be delivered tomorrow."

When she got home, she had phone calls to make.

"Mike?" she said, when he answered with a cheerful, "Mike's Diner."

"Hey, Lilah." He paused. "Everything okay there?"

She'd never phoned him before, and he sounded worried.

"Everything's great," she assured him. "I called because I want to give Daniel a surprise birthday party, and I'd like to know what you think about that."

"Great idea," Mike said. He sounded surprised himself. "It will embarrass the heck out of him. What can I do to help?"

Those few words made her feel amazingly good. "Thanks so much," she said gratefully, "but we think we can…"

"Come on. What we do here is cook. Maury and I can do some of it ahead of time and store it here."

"I have to admit that would be a big help." Daniel's brother being nice to her gave her the wonderful feeling that he'd accepted her. "Any ideas about what Daniel likes most? I'm still thinking about the menu."

"Sure, but it might give me a kick to present him with the things he likes *least*." Mike chuckled. "Come by the diner tomorrow afternoon when Maury's here and the lunch crush is over, and the three of us will put together a menu."

"Thanks," she told him. "I'll be there."

"How are you going to surprise him when he works right there in the house?"

She swallowed hard. "The boys suggested Ian might come up with a sick sheep. Daniel would run to the rescue and…"

Mike's chuckle escalated into a burst of laughter. "Let me know how the conversation goes," he snorted.

"I was hoping," her voice faltered, "you might ask him."

"Nope, you ask him," Mike said, and was still laughing when he hung up on her.

Then she had a brilliant idea.

"You want me to call Uncle Ian?" Nick said.

Lilah had surmised that Ian and Nick had some special bond, maybe because they were both so closed inside themselves. From Nick's smile when Ian picked up the phone, Lilah gathered that Ian hadn't growled. "We're gonna give Daniel a surprise birthday party."

Nick's smile grew wider. Then he said, "But you have to help. If we're gonna surprise him, you have to have a sick sheep." After a long pause, he said, "Because you live the farrest away and if you had a sick sheep he'd come, even on his birthday." Another pause. "Can you think of something else?" Another pause, and then, "Thanks, Uncle Ian. Lilah will call you to tell you the time and all that." Another pause, but this one was Nick's. "When are you coming over next?"

Nick had obviously liked Ian's answer. "He'll do it," Nick reported, his bright-green eyes shining. "He says he doesn't ever have any sick sheep and Daniel knows it, but he'll think of something else."

"Bless you, Nick," Lilah said, hugging him, and, seeing that Jonathan beamed as brightly as if she were hugging him. "You did it!"

"I like Uncle Ian," Nick said.

"We all like Uncle Ian," Jonathan said.

There was something in Ian that Lilah hadn't pene-
trated yet. She should work on it, and keep working on
her relationship with Mike, because if you married a
man, you married his family, too.

*Married?* Where had that come from?

"Mom, why are you blushing?"

"It's gotten so hot in here," Lilah said, and scurried
to the cleaning closet to get the furniture polish.

WHEN DANIEL WOKE UP from a restless sleep, his first
thought was about Lilah, how right she'd been about
winning over Ed and Virginia, how smart she was,
how…totally appealing.

His second thought was that Elmer Winslow was
bringing in his six-month-old husky mix to be neutered.
Funny that men acted so squeamish on these occasions,
while women seemed rather cheerful about it. He might
have to give Elmer a dose of the anxiety drug he kept
on hand in case somebody's pet panicked in the clinic
waiting room.

Last of all, he realized it was his birthday. Not just
his birthday, but his thirty-fifth birthday. The number
depressed him for a minute, then he thought about the
path he'd traveled in those thirty-five years.

He was the luckiest man alive was his conclusion,
and with that in his mind, and thoughts of Lilah half-
successfully shifted onto the back burner, he showered,
shaved and dressed in the best of moods.

Feeling ready to face the day, Daniel strolled into the
kitchen. Lilah turned from the stove to give him a brilliant smile and say, "Happy birthday! Jesse just told me."

"Happy birthday," Will said. He was already at the table, munching on dry cereal to stave off starvation until his real breakfast was ready.

"Thank you," he muttered. "Had to tell, didn't you?" he said to Jesse, who returned a defiant look from the counter where he was working.

Daniel looked at the counter. "Aw, no, Jesse, not a birthday cake. I want to ignore my birthdays. So you can just…"

Will pinned him down with soulful eyes. "*We'd* feel bad if you didn't have a birthday cake."

"Right," Jonathan said as he stepped into the kitchen with Nick a half step behind him. "And besides, birthday cake is good."

"It's chocolate," Will said reverently.

"You're not cutting it to look like a cow."

"I know at least that much," Jesse retorted.

Daniel grumbled some more and kept grumbling as Maury and Jason joined them and annoyed him with still more birthday wishes.

It was pure pleasure to vanish into the clinic, where life was calm and—clinical. As always, he kept an eye on the window to watch the boys' day shaping up. Lilah drove them to soccer camp this morning. Jesse was probably fixating on that darned cake.

Jesse brought them home at noon. Lilah was probably getting their lunch together.

Birthdays made him remember parts of his life he wanted to forget: made him realize he needed the comfort of predictability every bit as much as his boys did. Would he ever get past it completely? No. He could only remember it and then put it into the perspective of his life now, every day of his life.

Which he'd do right now. Spurred on by a delicious aroma, he stepped into the kitchen briefly to pick up something for lunch. He usually took it back to his office rather than eating with the boys in a preoccupied way. Lilah didn't even spare him a glance. She was too busy trying to keep up with the Philly cheese steak sandwich demand. He put one on a plate, turned down the offer of French fries and coleslaw, and took a minute to stroll through the house.

It had been amazingly clean and neat since Lilah took over. The boys still helped on Saturday mornings, but she'd taught them how to do it right. Today it was downright gleaming.

He sighed. If she took a notion to leave, his life and the boys' lives would take a severe downturn.

He wouldn't think about it. She was here. He'd enjoy it while he could.

Mike called to wish him a happy birthday. Daniel snarled, "Thanks." Just as he was thinking he might get away from the clinic early, Ian called.

"I need you to come out and take a look at my lambs. Oh, yeah, and happy birthday."

"Thanks. What's wrong with the lambs?"

"The lambswool didn't come up to standard this year. I had to sell it cheap. It's something they're eating, or not eating."

"Okay. When do you want me to come?"

"Right now."

"On my birthday?"

"Don't give me that bull—"

"Language."

"That bull. I know what you think about your birthday."

Daniel sighed. "Okay. I was about to close down, anyway."

Twenty minutes later, his fingertips were rolling through the wool on a lamb. "Feels good to me."

"Well, it isn't. The lanolin level's low. They're not getting enough…something."

"That isn't my field, really," Daniel said, rubbing the lamb behind its ears. He stood up, feeling the softness of his fingertips from the lanolin that Ian said wasn't there. "The health of the lambs is, and this one looks great."

Ian frowned. "At least come in and look at some catalogs. There are all kinds of vitamins and minerals that are supposed to increase fleece growth and improve quality, but I don't want anybody scamming me." He gave Daniel a pleading look that wasn't anything like Daniel's image of Ian. "If I lose my reputation with the buyers," he said, "I'm sunk. The corporation's income goes down. It affects all of us."

"Okay, I'll look at the catalogs with you, but I should be getting home soon. Hang on a sec." He called to say he'd be late and that the kids should go ahead with dinner, then followed Ian into his office.

He'd never seen the guy so chatty. Of course, sheep were his passion—sheep and managing money—and maybe he was equally chatty with other sheep herders and wool merchants. It was almost seven when he said, "I think we've got your order wrapped up. I really have to go. The kids will think I've abandoned them."

"Yeah," Ian agreed. "Thanks for the advice. Sorry I used up so much of your birthday."

"Sooner it's over, the better," Daniel said gruffly.

When he pulled into the driveway, everything was quiet. The boys were usually outside kicking soccer balls or pitching baseballs. They must have finished dinner, because the kitchen was dark. Lilah probably had them doing something like playing Scrabble. She wasn't hurting their spelling abilities any, that was for sure.

He pulled into the carriage house beside the van and strode toward the side door. They couldn't be playing games in the living room, because the downstairs was dark. Even though it would be light outside for another two hours, the shade of the maples made lights necessary by six. He glanced skyward. The upstairs was dark, too.

Oh, no. A power outage. With an eight-man household, a power outage was a crisis of the first order. That did it. He was getting the generator he'd been meaning to have installed for years. He dashed through the clinic door, then into the dark hallway. "Jesse, Lilah," he shouted. "No electricity?"

Nobody answered. Had they all been abducted? His heart thudding, he grabbed a baseball bat from a stone crock that stood at the bottom of the stairs and started his search in the living room. The door was closed. Cautiously he inched it open, holding the bat high, and rushed into the room.

The room suddenly lit up, a camera flashed, and as he recoiled, startled beyond belief, more people than he could count yelled, "Surprise!"

## Chapter Nine

"You sure caught me looking like a complete fool," Daniel said, staring at the screen, on which his picture, complete with raised baseball bat and mouse-sees-snake expression, was on display. "Thanks loads, you guys."

"You looked just like that," Virginia Galloway said. "The camera doesn't lie."

"You looked worse," Jason said. "The photo is actually kind of flattering." He turned from the laptop to give Daniel an evil grin. Melissa Wilcox stood behind him, and Daniel gazed at her in awe. How the heck could Ed have fathered a girl this polite, cute and sweet? Life was full of contradictions, or maybe somehow Ed had managed to woo and win a wife just like Melissa. How in the world could he have managed that?

"Who's responsible for all this?" Daniel asked, waving his arm toward the bustling scene.

"You know it wasn't my idea," Ian muttered.

"Accomplices do time, too," Daniel said, glaring at him. "Lambswool crisis, my eye. Mike?"

Mike shrugged and delivered a slow smile. "My roasted asparagus, but not, absolutely not my idea."

"Jesse?"

"Disobey the general? Never!"

An embarrassing number of guests were chortling at his photograph, but Lilah was just about the only one left of his adult "family" to accuse. "Your idea," he said.

Her idea, too, to win over Virginia and Ed, and here they were at his birthday party, of all things, with Melissa Wilcox's eyes shooting stars at Jason's moonstruck face. He wanted his eyes to shoot stars, too. He wanted Lilah's face to be moonstruck. He wanted her.

Which was why he had to stand here glaring at her. The entirety of him, heart, soul and inflamed body, needed that glare to hide behind.

But then he took another look at her. Her stomach was clenched so tightly she could have fit into Scarlett O'Hara's dress with the seventeen-inch waist.

"Will you ever forgive me?" she asked, sounding as if she really was worried.

His heart sent a smile to replace the glare. "It'll take time. Ten minutes, fifteen…"

She relaxed and returned the smile.

DANIEL COULD MANAGE A smile, but inside he felt sort of crumpled or melted, vulnerable, anyway. Mike and Ian seemed to sense that he'd withdrawn for a moment, was looking at the party from the outside, and they sidled over to him.

"We could have stopped her," Mike said, "but not without telling her stuff we don't want to tell."

"It might be a good idea for us to go through a couple of things like this," Ian surprised him by saying. "Might get a handle on some of that 'stuff' we all have."

"Examine my inner feelings? Get in touch with my feminine side?" But his voice cracked when he said it.

Each brother gripped his shoulder, then moved away.

Yeah, another step toward getting "a handle on that stuff." Now he had more "stuff" to get a handle on, the unnerving knowledge that he was falling for Lilah and falling hard.

He turned down the heat that suddenly flooded him, squared his shoulders and scanned the room, deciding which group to join next. The house was filled to overflowing. Groups clustered at, on and around the picnic tables in the yard.

The boys had been allowed to invite their friends. Jason was still in the living room with Melissa. Daniel could glimpse Maury in the kitchen, aiming a self-conscious, adolescent grin toward the same pretty girl who'd come to his party. Lilah had invited everyone in Churchill he'd ever met, plus some spouses he hadn't even seen before. She'd clearly had a lot of help with the guest list.

The food was stand-up fork food and it looked amazing. Maybe that's what he should do next, sample it, but he felt too tense to eat. Back to the original idea—pick a group to join and turn on the charm.

Before he could do that, however, someone jangled a bell—a cowbell, he thought. The people who were gathered outside came indoors until everyone was sardined into the living room, the hall and all the way up the staircase.

It was Ed Wilcox who stood in front of the fireplace, ready to speak. He held a large vase in his hand, and Daniel dreaded to find out what was in it. A hand grenade? Jason's thumb?

No, Jason was fine, standing close to Ed, with Melissa at his side.

"Folks," Ed said, "a lot of us men don't like presents, so Miz Lilah said on the invitation, 'No gifts, except contributions to the foster-care center we're building in the valley.'"

Wow. Ed had made a one-hundred-eighty-degree turn in the last week or so. He'd accepted the center, and he felt a part of it. He'd accepted Jason. Wilcox-wise, things were looking good. And what had Ed been talking about? Contributions to the center?

"So here's your present, Doc," Ed said, and crossed the room to hand Daniel the vase.

He peered inside and saw envelopes. Envelopes with checks in them, and cash. When he picked up an envelope that appeared to be filled with change, he recognized Nick's handwriting.

Stunned again, he gazed out at the assembled group. Several long, painful seconds went by before he could say, "I don't know how to say thank you in a way that will tell you how *much* I thank you," he said. He knew Nick's entire net worth in allowance savings was probably in that envelope. He held back his emotions. "A Maserati, fully loaded, couldn't make me as happy or as grateful as these gifts have made me."

He got himself out of the limelight, clutching the precious vase, and worked his way toward Ed. "Thanks," he said. "You're doing a great job for the center."

Ed didn't exactly beam. He looked at the floor and shuffled his feet. Same thing as beaming, when you were talking about Ed.

Virginia Galloway bustled her way through Daniel's well-wishers, dragging Reverend Galloway behind her and then thrusting him in front of her. "We've seen the light," the reverend said ponderously. "We're one hundred percent behind the project."

"Virginia," Daniel said, "I can't tell you how much I appreciate the work you're doing."

Then he caught Lilah's eye. She was watching him in the way she often did, trying to read his emotions. He crossed the room toward her.

"This is the best thing anyone has ever done for me," he said softly. "Especially the present."

"You needed a vase really badly," she said with a mischievous smile. "I'm glad you like it."

But her face shone with pleasure. She had no idea how much she'd already done for him. Turned his life around, that's what she'd done. He had a sidekick now, somebody to share things with. She'd offered Daniel the possibility of living a normal life, of finding a woman he loved enough to marry her.

In fact, he thought he'd found her.

"THERE WEREN'T ANY LEFTOVERS," Jason complained. He and Maury were doing KP duty, and the younger boys had been sent to bed.

"Just a few," Lilah said. "Aengus got a stingy-looking plate, and for some reason we have half a rhubarb pie, about a cup of sautéed brussels sprouts and a half cup of the celeriac remoulade."

"Clearly," Daniel said, "I'm the only one who liked those things. How did you know what I liked?"

"Jesse, Mike—especially Mike—and Ian. You think we didn't cook enough?" She looked worried.

"No, if we'd had any more food, everybody would still be here," Jesse declared. "I'm glad there weren't any left-overs. Made it easier to clean up. Daniel, get away from that pan. We said you couldn't help and we meant it."

Lilah noticed how gently Maury removed the pan from Daniel's hands. Looking resigned, Daniel sat down at the kitchen table.

"Thank the powers that be for paper and plastic," she said. The kitchen actually looked pretty neat. The dishwasher was already on its second load. The rest of the pans and serving dishes were rinsed and stacked on the counter, taking up the least amount of space possible, ready for the next dishwasher load.

"We're quitting," Jesse said. "I'll get up in the middle of the night and load the dishwasher again."

"I'll come over early and do it," Lilah said.

"You'll find it done," Jesse said, staring her down. He gave Jason and Maury a sharp salute. "Dismissed!" They fled, and then Jesse said to Lilah, "You, too, young lady."

"I'll walk you home," Daniel offered.

THE IDEA OF BEING ALONE with Lilah had been simmering in his mind all evening, and now it was at full boil.

A minute alone with her was all he needed to show her how he was coming to feel about her, how he felt about her after she'd done this for him, organized the party, which was so…what should he call it? Kind? Affectionate? Caring?

Loving? He had a hard time even thinking the word.

He still knew nothing about her past. He'd made many attempts to draw her out, which had netted him only a too-bright smile and zero information. Maybe she was hiding from the law. Jamison might not even be her real name. She might be a professional crook with a forged driver's license. She'd renewed hers just after she'd arrived, and he'd have given anything to see the old one, read the address on it.

But he, of all people, knew you had to share your secrets in your own time. He hadn't shared his deepest ones with her, either. Would he be able to someday?

A cool breeze blew her hair around her shoulders. In the moonlight it shone, honey shot through with gold. Her face was sweet. Yep, the perfect profile of a professional crook.

"I know I acted like a grump tonight," he told her. "But I think every man secretly wishes something like that party would happen for him."

"I figured that was the case," she said. She turned toward him, gazed at him for a heartbeat, then seemed flustered by whatever it was she saw in his face. Without a transition, she shifted her gaze to the sky.

"I haven't traveled much," she said cheerfully. "Just enough to know the stars are more beautiful in Vermont than anywhere else."

Daniel laughed at himself. She sounded like a professional crook, too. She'd given him an opening to ask questions about her travels, but suddenly he didn't want to. He just wanted to be with her, whoever she was.

What he wanted was to step five feet away from the kitchen door, pull her into the darkness and kiss her senseless. But he cautioned himself to go slowly, slowly, not scare her. So he looked at the stars with her. "There's the Big Dipper," he said.

"That one," she said, "looks like The Scales. I wish I knew them all. There's a children's book of the constellations I've been meaning to give Jonathan...."

"I know a lot of them," Daniel said, drawing a little closer to her. "There," and he pointed to a waterfall of stars, "is the Overturned Apple Cart, discovered in the seventeen-hundreds by a farmer with an orchard."

Her laughter traveled like a bell through the darkness. "I thought the Greeks and the Romans did the naming."

"No, no, that's an unfounded rumor. Truth is, most of the constellations were identified and named by sharp-eyed Vermonters who were standing out in the dark looking up."

Her eyes sparkled at him. "Okay, so what's that one?" She pointed to the Little Dipper.

He wanted to see that sparkle of fun in her eyes again. "Measuring Cup," he said confidently, "named by a wife who was thinking about how she had no business standing out here in the dark when she needed to be starting her bread dough."

"Fascinating," she murmured. "And that one?"

And then it just happened. She leaned into him, he put his arm around her. He knew what would happen next, knew it would change everything, and he was ready for the change. "That one," he said softly, "was named by a young man who'd met a girl at a dance that night and couldn't get her out of his mind. It's called The Kiss."

He leaned down to her and brushed his lips against her satiny cheek, heard her sharp hiss of breath, felt her hesitation, and then, with a deep sigh that might have meant anything, relief, resignation, she turned her face to his.

Her mouth was soft, warm and yielding. When she reached up to cup his cheeks, he closed his arms around her, held her tight, kissed her with all the hunger and need in his soul. She responded to him, her breath coming faster, her hands sliding to the nape of his neck to draw him closer.

He pulled her tighter, feeling the length of her body against his. It inflamed him. *Hold back, hold back.*

IN THE CIRCLE OF DANIEL'S arms, enraptured by his kiss, she floated in the purest pleasure and ached with the deepest agony. She shouldn't be kissing him. As long as she hid her rapidly accelerating desire for him, she could continue to hide her past. How could she spill out her feelings for him in a kiss, then deny him the truth about who she was, what she'd hoped to escape when she fled to the valley?

Her heart, her body, had taken over her mind. She wanted him, felt she'd burst if she couldn't have him, and everything logical and pragmatic had flown away on the wind.

She'd be sorry someday, but she couldn't seem to feel sorry now. All she could feel was his mouth on hers, the electricity generated by the flicker of his tongue, the ache of his aroused body against hers. She couldn't breathe normally, couldn't think sensibly, couldn't do anything except throw herself headlong into the moment she'd been waiting for almost from the day he'd charmed her and Jonathan into the warmth and comfort of his home.

A dog barked. Aengus. She felt Daniel shift gears just as she was doing; felt him break free of the magnetism that held them together. She was suddenly aware of lighted windows behind them, of a house full of innocent, trusting boys, including her own.

She slid her lips away from his. "Reality check," she said shakily.

She could feel his smile against her hair. "A houseful of chaperones." But he didn't let go of her.

"It's even possible that this was Aengus's watch and Jesse will take over in a minute."

"Yeah, and Jesse will ream him out for not sensing the danger sooner." He drew away, then cupped her cheeks and held her gaze with his. "Is there any danger here?"

"Oh, yes," she said, knowing he had no idea how much danger and still not telling him, unwilling to give up the moment. "And Aengus knows it. Think we could go with his judgment for now?"

For now. If she made love with Daniel, would the dog's barking—or silence—tell her all she needed to know?

Because it was Daniel's heart Aengus would be guarding, not hers.

AS HE'D PREDICTED, everything had changed. If Daniel had ever wished for a middle-of-the-night emergency, it was now, and, of course, every animal, large and small, was in great shape that night. Nothing to distract him from his aroused, heated state. He slept restlessly, dreaming of nothing but the feel of Lilah's body against his. When he made his appearance in the kitchen, he couldn't just say, "Pancake day!" His gaze met Lilah's and electricity sparked again, followed by renewed longing, and instead he said, "Hi," watching her face flush, before she turned back rapidly to the griddle where pancakes were browning.

"Good morning," she said, sounding short of breath.

"It's hot standing over the stove," he observed, moving up beside her. "I'll flip a few of those."

His arm brushed hers. He felt a shock wave pass through him, saw her blush deepen.

"Okay, thanks," she said, but she lingered a moment before she slipped away.

*No, it will never be the same.*

Jesse stood beside Daniel, turning bacon in the skillet, adding more crisp strips to the pile of them that was rising next to the stove. "You've finally come to your senses." He muttered the words, because the younger boys had just barreled into the kitchen.

"Or lost them," Daniel muttered back. He was grateful to have an extremely busy day ahead of him.

LILAH DIDN'T KNOW HOW she'd get through breakfast. Her body zinged with nervous energy. All night she'd moved restlessly between her sheets. When she slept, she dreamed of Daniel, of his kiss going on and on until there was only one way to end it, and then she'd wake up flaming with frustrated desire.

Walking to the house, she'd chanted a mantra: *I have a job. I have a son. I have a former husband lurking somewhere. I can't have this man until I've tied up the loose ends of my life.*

It was a kiss, just a kiss. But one look at Daniel and her mantra had turned into gibberish.

With Daniel flipping pancakes now, breakfast seemed to be under control, so she went to the make-shift office area in the living room, two long, narrow tables Daniel had found, which the boys had dragged down from the attic and placed at right angles. There she'd set up her work for the center. Now she stared down at the many drafts of visuals, at the file on the monitor, at the open DVD drive with the film in position on the disc without seeing any of it. Anything could happen, anytime. She had to have a full presentation worked up for Daniel before her life fell apart again. She could perfect it if the fates gave her time, but she had to give him something. Immediately.

Her mouth twisted. After breakfast. Stoically, she returned to the kitchen, to find breakfast ready and only one spot left at the table—on Daniel's right.

## Chapter Ten

Daniel had never been so relieved to retreat from the breakfast scene to the serenity of his clinic, the comfortable routine of his career. Sitting next to him, Lilah's body had seemed to throb with heat and her scent had dizzied him. It had been a struggle to be his normal, familiar self.

He couldn't let the boys see that anything was different between him and Lilah. His life might be changing, but theirs couldn't. They needed their ordinary routines and the promise of his reliability.

Still, at the high point of his day, his first reaction was to share it with Lilah. At his first break between patients, he burst through the clinic door, pounded toward the living room where he knew he'd find her working and yelled, "Lilah! Great news!"

She leapt from her chair, scattering papers everywhere, closed what she'd been working on with one swift click of the mouse and faced him, her eyes wide and blue.

"Sorry, sorry," he said, kneeling down to retrieve the papers.

"Hey, this is good," he said, examining a page of the handout.

"Forget the handout. What's the news?"

She sounded too cool for his comfort. He looked up to find her standing with her feet apart, her hands on her hips.

"I shouldn't have blown in here like that."

"You certainly blew my concentration," she said. "You owe it to me to tell me what's happened. Right now."

He was momentarily distracted by thinking how cute she was standing there pursing her lips. The heat rose stealthily inside him as his gaze skimmed over her cocked arms, slim and tanned in her simple white sundress. He picked up more of the scattered papers in an effort to remember why he'd stormed in here in the first place.

"I got a phone call today," he said. "Someone has volunteered to be the chief financial officer of the center."

"Volunteered? He'll do it for free?" Her hands went to her mouth. "Who is this saint?"

Daniel smiled. Her fit of pique had vanished, and she'd embraced his excitement. "He told me he 'did well,' that's the way he put it, in the construction business and had decided to take a few years away from that and use his skills to 'benefit others,' his words again."

"Daniel, that's wonderful!" She came around her desk, her eyes shining now. She was even more beautiful, more desirable than before. "What's his name?"

She was so close to him, and he was so distracted,

that he stammered, "T-Ted Hilton." He cleared his throat, which also seemed to clear his head. "I told him I'd call him when we had the board's approval and knew it was a done deal, then I went to the Web site he'd listed on his card. He's just what he said he was. The owner and CEO of Hilton Construction Company in Philadelphia."

"When can he come onboard?"

"Ten days or so, if the ship floats, so to speak."

"Wow!" She shone a brilliant smile at him. "No wonder you're so excited."

Their gazes locked. Her lips parted and her smile changed into one that was more personal, more for him than for his good fortune. Drawn beyond his resistance, he reached out to her. She tilted her head toward him.

"Doctor! Celia Hennessey is here with Otis." It was Mildred, yelling from the clinic door. He resented her timing.

Lilah drew back, her mouth curved in a wicked smile. "Thanks so much, Dr. Foster, for dropping by."

He regarded her gloomily. "Take two aspirin and call me." Then he smiled. "Any time, day or night."

"YES, I SHOULD BE WORKING," Lilah told Jesse, "but if I don't get out of the house for a while, I'll mildew."

"Okay," Jesse said, resigned in the face of Lilah's determination. "Here's the grocery list." He handed her two full handwritten pages he'd been about to take to the supermarket.

"We eat a lot."

"You noticed."

"So here I go. I'll be back by lunchtime."

She set off in her own car for the local supermarket in a lovely, shivery, anticipatory mood. She'd been on *The Kingdom Dispatch* Web site when Daniel surprised the heck out of her, and once again she'd seen no mention of Bruce, nor had there been an obituary for Mrs. McDougal. She could relax again, and however short these relaxed periods were, she appreciated each one of them.

But it had been the sight of Daniel popping in that had created the shivery, anticipatory mood. If only, if only…

Churchill being a small town, she hadn't had much time to agonize over the "if onlys" before she'd parked and prepared herself to empty the grocery store. Fortunately, the local supermarket was usually stocked for the frequent Foster onslaughts.

She snagged a cart and set off for the meat counter. Ground beef, tons of it. A stack of juicy chuck roasts that Jesse would turn into pot roast and a hefty stew. Pork country ribs. The boys loved them. Chicken.

She eyed the cart and wondered if she should leave this one by the checkout and start on another one. Daniel's household seemed to revolve around food.

She was sailing past the lamb, which Ian had banned from Daniel's menu and heading toward the bacon and sausage when she saw the florist poised over the cooler.

"Lilah!" the woman bubbled. "I'm so glad to see you. I should have called, but you know the flower business."

"Um, well…"

She shook her finger at Lilah. "What I wanted to tell you was that you forgot to sign the card when you sent those flowers. But don't worry. I did it for you."

Lilah's wonderful mood sank. Now Mrs. McDougal's son knew who'd sent the flowers. But on the other hand, what bizarre circumstance would cause Harold to tell Bruce she'd sent his mother flowers? And how many of her steps would Bruce have to trace in order to find her here in Churchill?

If anyone could do it, he could. Feeling like a lump of lead, Lilah forced herself to finish shopping, help Jesse put away the food, paper supplies and cleaning products, and greet the boys with her customary exuberance. Even a single, unimportant connection could end her comfortable new life here, the happiest life she and Jonathan had ever known.

FOR ONCE, GOOD NEWS followed good news, and when Daniel came in from the clinic that afternoon, he went directly to Will's room. "Will," he said, "talk to me a minute?"

At dinnertime, he made his big announcement. "Will's parents are doing so well with their physical therapy that the doctor says Will can go home in about a month."

Besides Will, who looked excited enough to pop, only Jason understood the full import of the news. "Will we ever see you again after you go home?" Jonathan asked mournfully.

"All the time," Daniel said. "At school, at Sunday

school, we'll invite him to all the family events, and he can come over anytime he wants to."

"We'll still be friends," Nick said to comfort Jonathan.

"And I'll always be here if you need me," Daniel said to Will.

He glanced around the table. Jason wore a half smile, happy that Will was happy but with no desire to have the same thing happen to him. If Maury, who was working at the diner, had been here, he would have reacted in much the same way. Lilah and Jonathan were studying each other, a mother and son who hadn't had to be separated.

Nick came last in Daniel's clockwise scan. In the boy's eyes, he saw a flicker of fear.

*Fear of what?* Daniel longed to know.

"Tonight we're celebrating," he said.

"How?" Will asked, undoubtedly wanting to know the menu rather than the activity.

"We're going stargazing." He flicked a glance at Lilah, watching the pink rise in her cheeks.

The boys gave him expressionless faces.

"At Uncle Ian's."

They perked up a bit.

"Build a bonfire and roast marshmallows," he concluded.

That got them excited. The room exploded into action. Aengus, knowing something good was about to happen, bounced through the chaos, barking frantically. Jesse began packing supplies.

Jason cleared his throat. "Could I, um, is it okay if—"

"If Melissa could come, too? Sure thing." He took it

seriously, didn't smile, didn't want Jason to feel he was being teased.

Jason went straight for the phone. Daniel caught phrases of his end of the conversation. "Tell your dad it's the whole family." After a pause, "By nine. It's the younger kids' bedtime."

He shuffled back toward Daniel. "She can go," he said casually. "I'll pick her up while you guys are getting your act together."

Daniel hid a smile. Apparently the answer had been yes.

Lilah stood to one side, smiling indulgently at the furor. "I'll stay here and clean up," she said.

"Don't even think about it," Daniel said. He put his arm around her and gave her a gentle push. "Get a sweater." He heard his voice hoarsen as he touched her. "See you at the van in five minutes."

A car pulled into the driveway. "Maury's home," Nick yelled. "He can go, too!"

DANIEL MUST HAVE KNOWN, just as Lilah did, that if he stargazed right beside her, it would be too much torture to endure. They all lay on blankets spread over the lush green grasses of Ian's acreage, coincidentally on the very spot where the center would—God and the Regional Development Board willing—rise over the next few years.

Jesse tended a bonfire he'd started in a huge metal barrel beside a sheepherder's shack. Will was more interested in the marshmallows than the stars and only paid attention occasionally when something in the conversation caught his attention.

Unbelievably, Maury, the worst student of all Daniel's boys, turned out to be the house expert on constellations. Soon everybody was searching for the star formations that he saw so easily.

Lilah smiled, thinking of Daniel's constellation expertise, and shivered, remembering his kiss. Jonathan lay beside her, looking at her occasionally, as if he was thinking about Will, who'd been away from his mother so long.

Nick and Will were on opposite sides of Daniel, with Nick as close to him as he thought he dared to be without looking babyish.

Jason, his head resting on Aengus's haunches, gazed up at the sparkling sky, probably wishing he was alone with Melissa, who lay a proper distance away. They hadn't touched each other all evening, behaving in front of the family as if they were just friends. They were thoughtful kids, both of them.

Maury, exhausted from his shift at Mike's Diner and his constellation lecture, had fallen asleep.

Ian leaned against the shack, his arms folded across his chest, not participating, just observing as he so often did.

Lilah closed her eyes for a moment. It was so tranquil. Was this the beginning of a worry-free life for her and Jonathan, or was it the calm before a violent, destructive storm?

*Enjoy the peace for now. It could be your last chance.*

"I'M GOING TO FAINT."

Daniel turned toward Lilah. She did look pale. In

white trousers and a blue silk shirt, the same shirt she'd been wearing the morning she'd joined their lives, she was lovely. She'd be lovely lying on the floor in a faint, too, but it wouldn't go over well with the audience.

"Calm down," he told her. "It'll wow them."

"Let's start then, and get it over with."

He smiled. "Ladies and gentlemen," he whispered to Lilah, "take your seats. The show will start in one minute."

She sat down, looking like the next in line on death row, and he stood before the audience. After a short introduction, he signaled for the film to begin.

It was smooth and beautiful, the rolling fields of Ian's farm gradually turning into a mockup of the center made with the architect's models. Ray had done a remarkable job. Lilah had had a brainstorm, and had conscripted Reverend Galloway to narrate the film. His sonorous voice vibrated throughout the packed room.

The film segued into scenes of the center in Connecticut, with children gathered at the table in one of the homes, playing baseball on a field with mountains in the background—just as they would on Ian's land—and gathered in the recreation room for a movie.

The last segment had been Ray's idea. "Need to shoot the reactions of the townfolks," he said, "then cut and splice to weed out the cuss words."

"Reverend Galloway would never, um, cuss."

He gave her a "where did you come from?" look. "This part will be a talkie."

They'd ended up with a balanced set of responses, from a gushing, "We love the feeling that our community is doing something good for these poor, abandoned children," to "What center?" which netted a laugh from the audience.

As for background music, the Churchill Consolidated High School band played a soothing and relatively recognizable version of "Climb Every Mountain." Daniel had suggested, "With a Little Bit of Luck," which had earned him a look from Lilah, the kind of look that made him smile each time he recreated it in his mind.

It didn't matter if the band was good. Every kid in that band had a parent or two, and they'd all come to the meeting.

When the film ended and the lights went up, the room was hushed. Then slowly the applause began, rising to a crescendo that rocked the room.

Daniel was consumed by elation. He didn't want to break the spell. Every element of the PowerPoint presentation was duplicated in the handout.

"I'll give you time to glance at the printed materials, and then I'll be happy to answer your questions."

There was only one question, and it came from Ed Wilcox. "I just wanna know how soon we can get going on this thing."

The board withdrew to vote. The center had its unanimous approval.

Daniel and Lilah said their goodbyes, then went to the van with impeccable propriety. As soon as they were inside, though, Daniel gripped her hand and raised it in a victory salute. "We did it!"

The powerful aura of success vibrated through the van. "You did it. Oh, Daniel, I'm so…"

He lowered their hands, putting hers to his lips. "We did it. You've been my inspiration."

He gazed at her, drew her closer. Excitement still hummed through him, spiked by desire. He started the engine, drove a few blocks, then said, "I'm too keyed up to sleep. Know what I want to do? Go to Ian's farm and walk the site."

Her soft voice throbbed through him like a jungle beat. "I'd like that."

They must have talked on the fifteen-minute drive across the river to LaRocque, then down the narrow road to Holman, but he couldn't remember what they'd talked about. He wasn't listening to anything but the music in his own mind, absorbing the scent of Lilah next to him and feeling the want and need surging through his body.

He parked beside the sheepherder's shack. It took all his self-control to get out of the van, take her hand and begin the walk across the dewy grass. The land seemed to stretch out into space just as the sky did.

"If I have my bearings right," he said, hearing his voice crack, "the main building should go up about here."

"And the houses in a circle around it, with gravel drives circling around from the main road to them and on to the…"

"The playing fields over there," Daniel murmured. "And…"

"Children everywhere," Lilah said. "Happy, having fun, getting over the sad circumstances that brought them here."

Her voice quivered. He couldn't hold back any longer. He spun her toward him, took her in his arms and pressed her face against his chest. "You made it all happen," he told her. "Not just the presentation tonight, or having the genius to catapult Reverend Galloway to stardom…" He felt her soft laugh against his chest. He pulled her tighter and laced his hand through the silk of her hair. "You gave me the support I needed to believe in myself and in the center. All of those things, they made my dream come true." He tilted her head to look into her eyes. "You are my dream come true."

Her lips met his with certainty this time, her need and his meeting in a flash of lightning that made their kiss sizzle with pent-up passion. It was a kiss filled with the joyous energy of flicking tongues, caressing hands, each body seeking the heat of the other. He trailed his mouth across the corners of hers, across her cheek to her ear, which he outlined with his tongue, relishing her soft moan and the way she went limp in his arms.

He slid his hands down to her buttocks, pulling her closer to his raging heat, fitting her to him, feeling her move instinctively against him. The sky lit up with electricity, and thunder rolled through him.

"Daniel," she panted, "I think that actually was thunder and lightning."

And the rain began to fall, huge drops splattering their heads. "Run to the shack," he told her, and together they raced to the little building, bursting through the door soaked and laughing.

HAD THE STORM SAVED HER from herself? What she was doing here wasn't fair to Daniel. She couldn't make love with him when she was living a lie. Or *had* it sealed her fate? She was more alone with him than she'd ever been, and she wanted him with a desperation she hadn't known she was capable of feeling.

While these thoughts spun frantically through her head, he wrapped a blanket around her and another around himself. They were the blankets they'd lain on as they stargazed on that recent night, and now a stack of them sat at the foot of a rustic bed.

Resisting Daniel would be easier if the cosmos weren't conspiring against her and providing a perfect place to make love. She shivered—from excitement rather than cold. She wanted nothing more than to be in that bed with Daniel. And she could read on his face, in his eyes, in the touch of his hands on her, that he wanted her just as badly.

*But he doesn't know the truth about me. He doesn't know I'm living a lie.*

"You're cold."

The low throb of his voice and his steady gaze were enough to warm her. When he wrapped his arms around her, he made her feel alive and cherished. He brushed her mouth with his, teasing her lips with his tongue.

Suddenly it wasn't like teasing anymore. Now he kissed her hard and deep, his hands moving over her back in an exquisite rhythm as his tongue explored her mouth. She slid her arms around his neck, too aroused to remember why she was supposed to be pushing him away. Thinking at all was impossible with Daniel touching her, so she stopped trying and let herself be a mindless creature of pure sensation, reveling in the joy of being close to him. She slipped the blanket off her shoulders, and in a second, his joined hers. Now they were much closer. It was better, but it still wasn't enough. She wanted him to surround her. She wanted him inside her.

She freed her lips from his and said breathlessly, "I think now is when you're supposed to say, 'We have to get you out of those wet clothes.'"

It was all the permission he needed. He groaned as he reached slowly for the top button of her shirt. One after another, the buttons slipped free until her blouse fell open. He leaned forward and kissed the valley between her breasts.

The sensual feeling of his lips on her skin made the last of her control evaporate. He must have felt the same way, because his breathing was ragged as they frantically tugged off clothes.

Just before the last garment dropped to the floor, he fumbled a condom out of his wallet. Then he picked her up, stretched her out on the bed and lay beside her, pulling her body over his. As he kissed her deeply, he also caressed her, running his hands over her skin until she was nearly insane with desire. At last she knew the whole of him, hot skin, muscular body, flat stomach, his intense need for her.

In her aroused state, she felt powerful. She sat up, straddling him. Never letting go of his gaze, she lowered herself onto his erection, melding their bodies, their hearts. She'd never believed in fate until now, but the sensation of being with Daniel was so perfect that she truly believed they were meant for each other.

Slowly she moved over him, savoring the sensations that were engulfing her. She knew she was pushing him to the edge of his willpower with her deliberate, provocative movements. He reached up to cup her breasts, his fingers teasing her taut nipples.

Unable to contain her desire any longer, she moved faster, faster, her breath coming in tight gasps. His hands moved to her hips, urging her on, pushing her toward the brink. With one last frenzied motion, she flew over the edge, the world exploding around her. She heard the deep, desperate groan that seemed to come from his very soul and collapsed onto his sweat-slicked chest, tingling with pleasure.

She lay there, both of them gasping for breath, for a moment, then she slid to his side, resting her head against his arm. "Wow," she murmured.

He drew her close. "Yeah. Wow."

All the reasons they shouldn't have made love flickered dimly at the back of her mind, but they were no longer important. Nothing mattered except what she felt for him, and what he felt for her. What problems existed could be resolved and overcome.

He shifted her to her back and smiled as he kissed her slowly, his tongue slipping inside her mouth, his leg slipping between hers.

"Yum," she moaned.

"Yum. Definitely yum," he said, and made love to her again, more slowly this time. When she climaxed, she felt as if her bones would dissolve.

In the deepening darkness she clung to him, deliciously sated at last. The rain had stopped. Thunder rumbled in the distance, matching the beating of their hearts.

Even if she could never have him again, she'd have this memory in her heart forever.

*Chapter Eleven*

She'd allowed herself those wonderful hours of love with Daniel and had relished the delicious dreams that followed it. In the morning Lilah confronted the fact that she'd made a selfish mistake, one she couldn't take back.

If only she could believe Bruce had given up trying to find her. If only she could give herself completely to Daniel without reservation. She'd known him for such a short time. How long had she been in love with him?

Until now, it had been a hopeless love. She wasn't in his league and she could never have *him,* just dreams of him. But now they'd kissed, touched, blended into one person. If she had to run away again she'd be left with, not merely dreams, but memories she'd never be able to forget.

She'd told Jonathan they were through with running away. She just hoped she could keep her promise.

She put on a cheerful face and went about her morning routine. When Daniel stepped into the kitchen, her heart thudded, her cheeks, her whole body flushed with heat. When he managed a kiss behind her ear in the split second they were alone, the ache of desire curling inside her was pure agony. She wanted to make love with him again and again and again.

Instead, her life seemed to consist of flipping pancakes, again and again and again.

When Daniel removed himself to the clinic, she felt as if he'd been torn away and had taken most of her with him. But by the time the boys were off to the pool, she'd managed to calm down and focus on reformatting copies of the PowerPoint slides that the head of Child Services would need for writing the first and most important grant proposal, which they'd submit to a well-endowed private foundation. The support of that foundation would be the bedrock of their fund-raising efforts.

Daniel came in for lunch with the boys. He seemed to be trying hard to treat her casually, but he wasn't succeeding any too well. His gaze kept meeting hers. She tried to look away, but found herself captured in his spell.

She had to rechannel both their minds before the boys began to notice that their behavior seemed different. "Has your new man, Ted Hilton, gotten here yet?" she blurted out.

"Got here today," Daniel said. He seemed as relieved by the distraction as she was. "He's pleasant, sounds smart and seems to know his job. He's already started setting up a budget for the construction. He's gone through the donor lists, targeted the ones he has some connection to and has estimated what they might donate."

"When do I get to meet him?"

"Soon, I hope. I suggested lunch tomorrow, but he has to meet with the architect."

"Well, I'm anxious to see what he's like," she said. "I know you shouldn't look a gift horse in the mouth, but..."

"I wouldn't look any horse in the mouth without protective gear." His eyes twinkled, and the vestiges of a smile hovered at the corners of his mouth.

Even the hint of a smile was enough to send her reeling.

Jonathan, whose gaze had been ping-ponging from her to Daniel while they talked, suddenly dropped his fork, a rare occurrence during a meal for any of the boys, and was staring at Daniel with his mouth hanging open. "Do they bite?"

Now Daniel had the full attention of the younger boys. "Sometimes," he said. "You and a horse can get to know and love each other, but some of them are skittish. Something scares them, they might throw you off, kick you or even bite you." His eyes moved toward Lilah. "Treat 'em nice. That's my advice about horses."

She knew what he was saying. They'd gotten to know each other, and she had come to love him. Was he waiting for her to get scared and throw him off, kick him or even bite him?

"Kids at school, mainly the girls, ride horses and think it's cool," Will said.

Jason and Maury, who'd been talking, tuned in. "Girls and horses," Maury said, shaking his head.

"Why do you think it's girls who like to ride?" Nick said. "In the westerns on TV, it's the cowboys riding the horses."

"Because it was their transportation then," Jason said, his smile so like Daniel's that Lilah had to catch her breath. "Women rode them for fun. Now," and he paused to beat his chest with his fists, "us guys have wheels, man. Who needs a horse?"

"Now the girls ride for fun and think you only need a car for transportation," Maury said, shaking his head. "Especially the town girls, who drive out to where they ride the horses."

"You got it," Daniel said, openly laughing now. The conversation was off and running.

Lilah sat back and listened. She was perspiring. True, the old house didn't have air-conditioning, but it had walls like a fortress, plus ceiling fans, so it rarely felt hot. It wasn't even hot outside, only a balmy seventy-five degrees. She was being tortured by the heat within, so to speak.

Too many things tortured her, invading her dreams and her daydreams both. Her love for Daniel. Her dread that Bruce would find her. Her fierce protectiveness of Jonathan. Why couldn't she just relax and admit that life was good right now, enjoy the moment and deal with the letdown when it happened?

Because she was so certain it would happen, and she had to be ready for it.

DANIEL WAS TRYING TO concentrate on his patient, a Yorkshire terrier so small you could miss him on the chair you were about to sit in, but he was distracted by noise in his backyard. A soccer game, sure, but louder than usual, with more shouting. He handed the Yorkie back to his owner with a comforting "Healthy as can be," and sped to the scene.

Yes, it was a soccer game, but the difference was that this time Lilah was playing along with the boys. Jesse was acting as referee, and Jason, back from work on Ian's farm, had joined in. They whooped and yelled as they raced across the grass, kicking and passing the ball with a fair amount of skill.

That didn't surprise him. What surprised him was Lilah. She'd never played soccer with the boys before, and since they were stopping now and then to show her how to make a move, he quickly realized it was because she didn't know how to. But she surely did look determined.

He had to give the boys credit. They seemed more interested in coaching her than in worrying about which team was winning.

"Shoot the ball, Mom," Jonathan yelled. "Shoot it into the goal really hard."

Lilah took aim and kicked, but she only grazed the ball, so it spun off to the side.

"I'll never learn to play soccer," she told them.

She was wearing navy shorts and a blue-flowered T-shirt. Her hair was pulled back in a loose ponytail, and her cheeks were flushed with exertion. He'd never seen a more beautiful woman.

When she saw him, she held his gaze for a long moment. The way she looked right now, wild and reckless, struck a blow to his midsection. She'd come to mean so much to him in such a short time. How had he gotten so lucky?

She came toward him. "I stink at this game."

"You have to focus on what you want. Then go after it." Her eyes sparkled. He could tell she'd read his meaning. His gaze slid down to her lips. What wouldn't he give to kiss her right now, in front of the boys, Jesse, the whole world? The desire was so strong, it was all he could do to hang on to what little self-control he had left.

Lilah blushed, as if she knew what he was thinking. Rather than looking away and breaking the spell, she met his gaze straight on. "Sounds like good advice. And what I want right now is to learn to kick."

With some effort, he stepped back from her and pointed at the soccer ball. "Stand directly in front of it and kick it squarely in the center."

She did as he said, and kicked the ball with such ferocity that it startled him. Again, she missed the net. "I'm hopeless," she said.

"You're…delightful," he said so softly that only she could hear.

Her lips parted. The air around them seemed to crackle with attraction. He'd never felt this way about a woman before. His love was all-consuming.

"Watch out, you two," Jesse yelled. "If you're not playing, then move."

He and Lilah had both stepped back a couple of feet when the ball flew into the air and headed directly toward them. Daniel moved out to intercept it, but before he could, Lilah ran forward and slammed it with her right knee.

The ball soared across the yard, flying into the make-shift goal so hard it knocked the net flat. For a second, they all stood still, amazed. Then Jonathan shouted, "You did it, Mom. You made a goal!"

The other boys began to cheer. Lilah held up her fingers in a V, smiled her thanks, then turned to Daniel. "Pure luck," she said. "Who knows if I can ever do it again."

"I do," Daniel said, longing to hug her. It was pure luck that she'd fallen into his life. A woman like Lilah wouldn't happen to him again. So he was going to keep her, no matter what it took.

THE SUPERMARKET HAD BECOME Lilah's social club. She spent so much time and so much of Daniel's money there that it was rare not to run into someone she knew. Ahead of her in the Baking Time aisle, she saw a dark-haired woman who looked very professional in a tan skirt and top with a white blazer.

"Dana," she said, pleased to see her. "I didn't know you had time for grocery shopping."

At the sound of her name, the head of Child Services whirled, and seeing it was Lilah, gave her an oddly hesitant smile. "Now and then, my husband reads me the riot act and insists on food in the house."

Lilah nodded. "Men are like that. They don't understand eggs and toast for dinner."

"And don't tell me he should share the shopping, because we decided to get along with one car—which I have."

It was just pleasant small talk, so why did Dana seem increasingly nervous?

"Lilah," she said suddenly, "do you have a few minutes to talk to me this afternoon?"

"Of course." Now she felt uneasy. "I'm going to the center volunteers' meeting at three—can you make it?"

"Unless there's an emergency. Right now I have to run the groceries home."

"Me, too."

"What about two o'clock?"

"Sounds fine."

Jesse came around the aisle with a second shopping cart. "Sale on spareribs," he told them both, and pointed to a tall stack of plastic-wrapped packages that were kept in place by an equally tall stack of pork loin roasts on the bottom and chicken parts on the top.

"I'd better get some—if you've left any," Dana said, smiling at him in the genuine way she'd smiled at Lilah in the few times they'd met before today, and whisked toward the meat section at the back of the store.

Lilah finished the shopping trip in a fog of worry. Dana was always so pleasant and kind. She doubted, somehow, that grocery shopping had made her lose her smile. Were there problems with the financial projections she'd given Dana? Something was certainly wrong.

She left Jesse with the job of putting away the groceries, telling him she needed to supply Dana with more information for the grant proposal, and almost sick with unease, she went back into town.

Dana was waiting with a pitcher of iced tea and a plate of cookies, but her eyes were worried and her mouth drooped at the corners.

"What's wrong?" Lilah said quietly. "Just tell me."

Dana sighed. "I got a letter this morning from the group of former foster children who intend to form a foundation to collect money for the center. Did Daniel tell you about them?"

"Yes. It's very good of them to want to pay back. But?"

"They sent me a letter, telling me they'd received it from someone who claims your husband isn't dead. That, in fact, Bruce Jamison was imprisoned for a fraud in which you participated fully, that might even have been your idea. According to the letter, he took the rap for you."

Lilah was suddenly stifled by the air in Dana's office. She could hardly breathe. Her worst fear had become a reality. Bruce had found her, and this was how he'd chosen to pay her back, by spreading rumors that would discredit her. If the valley residents believed those rumors, she'd have to leave the valley and start all over. Maybe he thought he could make her feel helpless enough to come back to him.

It wouldn't work. She wouldn't let him destroy her. He couldn't make her feel helpless any more. She and Jonathan had lived on the edge for more than three years, and she'd never once thought of going back to Bruce. Tears of anger and frustration filled her eyes and threatened to pour down her cheeks. "May I read it?"

Dana handed her a copy of the letter. Was she afraid Lilah would grab the original and run? She read slowly, her anger building. It was worse than she'd imagined, pompous, sanctimonious, and she could hear Bruce's voice in every line. It ended: "Jamison sinned, knew it, admitted it and paid for it. Ms. Jamison sinned, decided she didn't want to face the consequences and turned Jamison in. Is this the sort of person who should be caring for children?"

She halted, and her heart almost stopped beating. Clearly, Bruce even knew she was working for Daniel. He knew about Daniel's foster boys. She'd brought danger into all of their lives.

"I find this letter hard to believe," Dana said. "We ran a criminal background check when Daniel first hired you. Everything was fine."

"Have you discussed it with Daniel?" Was that her voice, so rasping and uneven?

"I'll have to, of course, but I wanted to talk to you first. Are these accusations true?" Dana looked as sick as Lilah felt.

"It's true that my former husband is alive. I lied about that because I'm afraid of him and didn't want to do anything that might help him find me. It's true that he's been in prison. It's also true that I turned him in. But I did *not* participate in his scam and would never have dreamed up a fraud of any kind." She was shaking with anger.

"I couldn't imagine you had," Dana said. "But I have to know that you're fit to be so involved with Daniel's boys." She paused. "And I also want to make sure you're able to take care of Jonathan."

Delivered sympathetically, it was still the worst threat Dana could possibly have made. "Will you let me tell Daniel about the letter?"

"You're in love with him, aren't you?" Dana's voice was soft now, gentle and understanding.

"I think so."

"I don't want him to get hurt."

"I would never hurt him," Lilah said, "but nothing in the world would make Bruce happier."

"Tell me about him."

Lilah sighed, getting control of her anger. "I was very young when I married Bruce. I'd grown up on the edge of poverty with parents who weren't happy together, and when this attractive, obviously well-to-do young man arrived in Whittaker—that's where I'm from—I saw him as my salvation. He moved me out of my parents' run-down house into a beautiful old one that we restored, got me out of thrift-shop clothes and into nice ones, and for a while I was happy beyond belief."

"I can understand that," Dana said, nodding.

"But soon after Jonathan was born, he changed." She felt sick, remembering how uneasy she'd been at the time. "He was tense, belligerent. He was in the construction business, and he'd decided to go on his own with a housing development in Whittaker. There was a beautiful property on the lake, where he was going to sell building sites and then proceed with construction. He said I should realize that he was worried about money—he had plenty of capital to make a down payment on the property, but he'd need to sell those sites to get loans for construction."

A slight frown appeared on Dana's forehead. Lilah didn't know what she'd said to cause that frown, but she kept going.

"He said I'd have to do his bookkeeping, in order to

save money. That was fine with me. I took a basic course in bookkeeping at the community college and then took over his financial records. But soon…"

"When money got tight, he took it out on you."

"How did you know?" She'd felt so hot a few minutes ago, and now she began to shiver.

"It's a familiar story in my profession," Dana said. She leaned forward, and the gaze she fastened on Lilah was penetrating. "My guess is that first it was yelling, then pushing, and finally hitting."

"You guessed right," Lilah said shakily. "Jonathan…" she bit her lip, fighting back tears, "witnessed a couple of incidents. The first time he tried to get between me and Bruce, tried to protect me. He wasn't even three yet. It broke my heart. No child should ever have that kind of experience."

"It's a credit to you that he's such a well-adjusted child."

"It's a miracle," Lilah said. "He's everything to me."

"When did you actually leave Bruce?"

"When he began selling the sites and we did have money, his attitude toward me didn't change. It was as if he wanted me to be afraid of him. As I got madder at him, my eyes got sharper. He's a great salesman and at last quite a lot of money was rolling in, but he wasn't doing anything with it except stashing it away. No architects' fees. No negotiations with contractors. No applications for loans to begin construction. It was pretty clear he was just accepting the money and had no intention of building the houses.

"When I confronted him, he…hurt me, threatened me, warned me to keep quiet. But I went to a lawyer, got his advice and then turned Bruce in."

"That took a lot of courage."

"I took Jonathan with me. I was scared to death that Bruce might—" She halted, feeling that fear again.

"I understand," Dana said, and this time she spoke gently.

"I didn't divorce him until after the trial. I didn't want to have to testify against him. But after he was sentenced, I insisted on the divorce. No settlement, because all the money we had went to pay back investors." She paused to square her chin. "It wasn't quite enough. I made up the rest from our savings, cashed in our insurance policies, sold the house, took a nursing job and kept just enough for Jonathan and me to scrape by."

Dana winced. "Then he got out of prison and you ran."

"Yes." Did Dana believe her?

"I'll have to think this over," Dana said. "I believe you, but we still have to do some investigating."

"Of course," Lilah said. She'd been hoping Dana would absolve her on the spot, but apparently it wasn't going to be that easy.

"You will tell Daniel." It wasn't a question.

"I'll skip the meeting and tell him as soon as he has time to talk to me."

Outside Dana's office, still shaky, Lilah flipped open her cell phone and dialed Jesse. "Jesse, there's something I have to do. How easy is dinner going to be? Yes, grill those ribs. Sounds great. Maybe we could grill the corn, too. Because I need to ask you a favor. Would you have time to go to the pool and keep an eye on Jonathan? He…he was a little sniffly this morning. I don't want him get too tired." She listened. "No, nothing's wrong," she lied. "It's just a bad connection. And Jesse, is Daniel in the clinic or making farm calls?"

Daniel was at the volunteer meeting. She'd have to go now. It would be agony waiting for it to be over. How would he react? Would he be shocked, horrified, or would he hold her close and tell her he believed in her, that everything would be all right?

She was sick at heart. Bruce had figured out the right people to target with that letter full of lies. He had probably figured everything else out, too, including the kids' schedules and their activities. She wished Jonathan were with her and not at the pool, but Jesse wouldn't let any strange man, anyone, for that matter, take Jonathan away.

Shoulders squared, she walked to the church where the meeting was being held. On the way, she ran into Virginia Galloway, who spoke politely enough but gave her an odd look as she scurried on toward the church.

Lilah's stomach cramped. Surely not...

She made her way down the stairs to the basement, a large room with a small stage at one end. The local pediatrician passed her on the stairs, giving her no more than a brief nod. At the bottom of the stairs, Sarah McNally, principal of the LaRocque Elementary School, turned away instead of speaking. Everyone turned away from her, until the mayor of Holman, a beautiful young woman from a political family, came directly toward her, gave her a sympathetic look and put an encouraging hand on her arm.

How many people had gotten that letter? Dana had

spoken as if she'd been the only one. Having no idea whom she might safely sit beside, she found a chair at the back of the small group and tried to make herself invisible.

For the first time, she didn't light up inside at the sight of Daniel. He didn't seem to see her. Maybe she *was* invisible. She half heard his encouraging speech to the volunteers. Behind her, she heard the door open and close, indicating that another volunteer had made it to the meeting, but she didn't turn around. She couldn't stand the possibility of another cool stare from someone she'd begun to think of as a friend.

She sank into her own thoughts. Terrible thoughts. If other people in the valley had already seen the letter, and believed Bruce's lies, she'd have to uproot Jonathan right now and leave without trying to defend herself. She'd lied to them about Bruce, told them he was dead. She could almost hear them saying it: "Lie about one thing, and she'll lie about another."

Worst of all, statewide child services wouldn't trust her to care for Daniel's boys. Maybe Daniel wouldn't trust her, either.

What if they tried to take Jonathan away from her? It was a thought too horrible to bear.

As soon as the meeting ended, she'd tell Daniel it was imperative that they talk immediately. For now, she had to wait. In spite of her worry, she finally managed to tune in to what Daniel was saying.

"I'm proud to introduce a new volunteer who has offered to be the financial manager for the center. A businessman himself, he brings his expertise to our project, temporarily deserting his own business, which is an act of great generosity. Ted Hilton, will you step forward, please?"

From a spot directly behind Lilah, a man moved confidently toward the stage. He turned to face the audience, and Lilah found herself looking at Bruce.

# *Chapter Twelve*

Lilah felt as if she'd been thrown overboard into the deep waters of the Atlantic. Her blood ran cold, her fingertips were icy. Struggling toward the surface, running out of air, she listened to Bruce deliver an exemplary speech, thanking all the volunteers, telling them how much he looked forward to working with them. He said the words looking straight at her. She felt certain that she, and only she, could see the hint of malevolence behind his polished smile.

Bruce did have talent. He was, beyond doubt, a superb con artist.

The meeting ended with a few final words from Daniel. Lilah made a beeline for him, but she wasn't as swift as Virginia Galloway. She and Daniel exchanged a few words that made Daniel nod soberly, then several other volunteers followed. She hung back, waiting her turn.

"Lilah."

Bruce's voice. She stopped in her tracks.

"Be with you in a minute," he said, smiling at several obviously smitten volunteers who'd surrounded him, "but someone told me this is Lilah Jamison, and we haven't met yet. Give us a minute."

She turned to face him. He held out his hand and smiled, performing for his public, but when he spoke, his words were for her alone.

"It's been a long time, Lilah."

"Not long enough," she spat at him, not caring who heard her. "What are you trying to do to me?"

Now his smile was the one she remembered all too vividly, cold and cruel. "You blew the whistle on me. Now I'm blowing the whistle on you."

"But I haven't done anything."

"Apparently you haven't read the letter that's circulating around the valley."

She clenched her fists. "Lies, and you know it."

"You lied about me," he said in a singsong voice, "and now I'm lying about you. Fair's fair."

"You—"

"Now, now," he said in a gently chiding way, "hear me out. I have a plan."

"To hurt me as badly as you can."

"Oh, no. To help you."

He couldn't con her any more. She didn't answer, just waited to hear more of his lies.

"Too bad about the letter," he said with false sympathy. "The townspeople will shun you. Saint Daniel," he hooked a thumb toward the stage, "will fire you. But I will resign from my exalted position, outraged at the community attitude toward you, and whisk you and Jonathan away from the scandal to an upper-middle-class life in, um, Pennsylvania."

"Forget your plan. Stay away from me," she said fiercely, "and don't get anywhere close to Jonathan, or Daniel, or his kids. Jonathan and I would go on welfare before we'd leave town with you. When I tell these people who you really are…"

The smile stayed in place, but his voice was like an icicle, sharp and cold. "Cooperate with me, Lilah. Don't even think about blowing my cover. You'll be sorry if you do."

He stepped away from her, and without missing a beat said jovially, "Sorry about that, ladies. Now I'm all yours."

Lilah made her way toward Daniel, but now she moved more slowly. Bruce had threatened her if she told anyone who he really was. But she'd told Dana the truth about herself and had promised to tell Daniel. Almost, not quite, as a condition of being regarded as a fit mother for Jonathan.

Threat or no threat, she *would* tell Daniel. The person she most needed to tell him about now wasn't herself, but Bruce.

Behind her, Lilah could hear him saying, "I got lucky with some investments, which gave me the capital to start the company. Then it did well and I…"

And, "I'd be happy to offer financial advice. I follow the market closely, and I…"

She had to drive him out of Churchill before he did irreparable harm to the community. She hurried toward Daniel, who saw her and ended the conversation he'd been having with the pediatrician.

"Daniel, I have to talk to you."

"Seems like everybody wants to talk to me right now, but you first," he said.

He whisked her out of the church and into the red pickup. Lilah saw no sign of Bruce. "So let's talk." He sounded busy—or harried.

"I…I have a lot to tell you." Her voice shook. "I want to show you something. Just drive. I'll tell you how to get there."

They made the trip in silence, except for the terse directions she occasionally gave him. At the end of the logging road, she said, "We're here." She turned to face him. "This is where Jonathan and I lived—until we met you."

She led him to the fallen tree trunk where she and Jonathan had spent so many hours, reading, talking, living on sandwiches and cereal. The memories of those two weeks were so painful that she hated to relive them, but Daniel had to know everything.

"What I have to tell you may change everything between us."

He raised his eyebrows.

"I'm not the person you think I am. I've lied to you. I've lied to the whole community."

His expression changed completely. "I know," he said. "I got the letter, too." His voice was calm, but in his eyes she saw that he felt betrayed.

"It was full of lies," she said, longing for that look to go away.

"Your husband isn't alive?"

"He is. I lied about that because it was a gentler story

than the truth," she said, shaking with anxiety. "Jonathan and I were hiding from him."

"Why?"

Dappled sunlight shot through the tall trees, mocking her sadness, her bitterness, as the dam that had held back the truth inside her burst and the words flooded out of her.

Daniel listened, his face tight. She found herself stumbling over her words, sounding, probably, just like a person who was telling a lie.

When she told him that Bruce had hit her, his expression changed briefly, encouraging her. "He gave you that scar," he said.

"Yes. When he found out I'd turned him in, he hit me with a cast-iron frying pan. Jonathan was there, screaming." Tears flowed down her cheeks at the memory. "I could hardly stand up, but I made myself stay awake and alert. I had to, to protect Jonathan. Bruce rushed out of the house, maybe thinking he could get out of town in time, but the police caught up with him. They stopped him for speeding, of all things, and as soon as he handed over his driver's license, they knew who he was and they took him in."

"He was a brute," Daniel murmured. "He could be dangerous to my boys, too."

"I thought I'd escaped him," she said, beginning to sob uncontrollably. "I was going to tell you now, tell you I have to leave, and tell you—"

His eyes were sad. "If you leave, you'll change all our lives. You charmed Jesse, the boys love you, and I..." he hesitated, "I love you."

Her breath caught.

"Until you, I'd never met a woman I trusted enough to love. See," he said, with such pain in his face that her heart wrenched, "I wasn't always the person I am now. Learning to trust has been the hardest struggle of my life."

"I'm so sorry," she whispered. "So sorry."

"I'll take you back to town." His shoulders drooped.

"I'll leave with Jonathan tonight."

"I guess that's what we'll have to do." He sighed. "Because of my boys. But not tonight. I don't want you driving with Jonathan when you're upset."

His instinct to protect Jonathan as well as his boys touched her. "Tomorrow, then. But I have one more thing to tell you."

Her heart had turned to stone, but it allowed her to calm down enough to deliver her biggest blow. "I didn't know until today, but this con artist, this violent man, was going to handle the cash flow of the center. Ted Hilton, your new financial manager, is my ex-husband, Bruce. You have to get rid of him."

His shock built to rage that was frightening in its intensity. "Because you lied to me, I was going to let this…this con artist, this violent man, handle the cash flow of the center?"

"That's not my fault! I didn't know he was doing this. I told you I wanted to meet him. Now I've met him, I've told you, and I assume you'll get rid of him."

"Damned right I'll get rid of him," Daniel said, suddenly sounding angry.

*And you'll be rid of me tomorrow morning, too. All's well that ends well.*

## Chapter Thirteen

Lilah huddled in her car, trying to calm down before she drove back to Daniel's house—for the last time.

Her heart was breaking, but she *had* to stay calm, cold as ice inside, until she'd done what she had to do. She had to tell Jonathan, and she'd decided she'd tell him the truth. She had to pack up her possessions. She had to give her son time to say his goodbyes, maybe have dinner with the family as usual and spend the night with Nick. She knew Daniel wouldn't punish Jonathan for his mother's sins.

Her sins. She'd handled everything so badly, when she'd thought she was doing just the opposite. Why had she decided to remain silent, try to be a different person in this new community? Fear of Bruce was a big factor, certainly. Pride? She didn't want anyone to know the kind of man Jonathan's father was. Didn't want anyone to know that she'd let that man abuse her verbally and physically.

It wouldn't help to beat herself up. It was over. She and Jonathan would run again. This time they'd have more money—she'd saved most of her salary, and they should be able to afford some sort of shelter. She should choose a larger city this time, in a state other than Vermont, would change her name.

They'd survive. But she was afraid they'd never be as happy as they'd been here.

The ice in her heart threatened to melt into tears. She took a deep breath, then started the car. She'd drive to the pool first, make sure Jonathan was all right, maybe even take him home with her. He'd protest, wanting to stay with Nick and Will, then ride his bike home—with Jesse driving right along with them.

Every thought that came into her mind reminded her of some moment during her stay with Daniel. Now she was remembering the family council Daniel had held to decide if the younger boys would be allowed to ride their bikes to the pool. He'd insisted that they be chaperoned everywhere, explaining to Lilah that sometimes the parents of foster children tried to get them back without going through proper channels, kidnapping them, effectively. And often the children went with them willingly, imagining everything would be all right. Especially with the mystery of Nick's past, Daniel couldn't take any chances, even if the boys thought he was overprotective.

But when they told him everybody in town rode their bikes to the pool except them, he'd been forced to realize that it was something that made them different from the other kids, the very thing he had struggled to avoid. So the compromise was bikes plus a grown-up in the caravan.

Sadness rose up inside her. It had all been so wonderful, and now it had come to an end.

She reached the pool just as Jesse drove away slowly in the van with three young cyclists following him in single file. Lilah pulled up behind them at a safe distance. This afternoon they'd be sandwiched in between two bodyguards. In her rearview mirror, she glimpsed another car she'd seen parked on the street beside the pool. She felt sorry for the driver. Passing two cars and three boys on bicycles would be dangerous on this narrow, curving road. He or she would be traveling at five miles an hour until the Foster cortege got home.

Home. Not her home anymore. She gritted her teeth. She had to gear up for the talk with Jonathan, which she was dreading more than she'd dreaded anything in her life.

DANIEL HADN'T MADE AFTERNOON appointments because of the meeting. When he got home, he saw that Lilah's car wasn't there. Maybe she was following the boys home from the pool. Or maybe she picked up Jonathan and left in spite of her promise to wait until tomorrow. Aching inside, he strode into the house, needing badly to spill out his anger and sorrow to Jesse, then make plans to increase security around the house until they were sure Bruce Jamison had left town.

Jesse wasn't there, either. Frustrated and let down, he got out Bruce's business card and dialed the man's cell number. Bruce didn't answer. Daniel left a deceptively polite message for the nonexistent Ted Hilton, then glanced at the card again.

If Lilah was telling the truth, there was no Hilton Construction Company in Philadelphia. So he'd call the number and see what he got. What he got was an "invalid number, please redial." He redialed, and got the same message.

So she *was* probably telling the truth about Bruce. Just a little too late. A lot too late, in fact. He sank into a kitchen chair. He'd known better than to let himself fall in love, and he'd gone ahead and done it anyway. He should have listened to Mike and Ian.

He grew angrier as he sat there. He dialed Bruce's cell number again, and this time he said, after the beep, "Bruce, I know who you are." *Anger won't help,* he reminded himself. *Sound like a man in charge, a fearless man.* "Leave the valley immediately and don't show your face here again. Lilah and Jonathan are under close surveillance." Right. He had no idea where Lilah was, and Jonathan was under the surveillance of a seventy-five-year-old man and two young boys. "You can't touch them. The chief of police knows about you," or would in a minute, "and I imagine your parole officer in Whittaker is expecting a visit from you. If you don't do exactly as I say and get out of here, the chief can get you on a parole violation. So leave, *now!*"

He dialed the police station and filled in the chief. "Nothing to charge him with yet," Daniel said, "but if you can find anything to pick him up for, do it."

He slammed the receiver onto the cradle, then picked it up again and called Dana at home. "Daniel, I'm so sorry," she said. "This is such a mess. I strongly feel that Lilah couldn't have—"

"Dana, Lilah *could* have done anything. She's been lying to me from the start."

"Daniel, are you sure?"

"The man who wrote that letter is her ex-husband, Bruce Jamison, an ex-con, who is currently calling himself Ted Hilton, the center's new volunteer financial manager."

There was total silence at the end of the line. Finally Dana said, "Well, Daniel, I've spent the past two hours trying to check out Lilah's story, so now I have information to refine the search." She hesitated. "Have you and she talked?"

"Yes. She says she had nothing to do with his scam and that he was brutal to her. And maybe he was. She has an ugly-looking scar on her forehead, says he hit her with a cast-iron pan."

"I believe her," Dana said. "Give me time to check out both of them."

"Let me know what you find. I know the guy's an impostor and there is no Hilton Construction Company, but is there any reason to think he's dangerous?"

"And Lilah? Do you think we might need to take Jonathan away from her?"

All the energy went out of him. "No, he loves her. He couldn't be faking it."

"Take it easy, Daniel," Dana said, and her voice was gentle. "We'll figure out the truth."

"She's leaving in the morning," Daniel said, feeling worse and worse. "I told her to."

Another silence, then, "I guess I have a lot of work to do tonight." Dana was brisk now. "Okay to wake you up if I have news?"

"I won't be asleep," Daniel said, because he knew it was true.

He began to pace the floor, waiting. Waiting for the phone call Bruce would never return. Waiting for Lilah, who would never come home to him again.

LILAH WAS BARELY AWARE she was driving as she followed the boys down the shaded road to the older part of town and Daniel's house, which faced another wooded area. It was a beautiful setting. Elderly neighbors on both sides, and a view of parkland across the street. She'd miss that, too.

The driver behind them was keeping a respectful distance from her car. A nice person. Maybe had a child in the car, too. Although she had her gaze focused on the boys, she was lost in wistful thoughts when the house loomed ahead, fanciful outside, comfortable and loving inside.

It happened so fast. The car behind them suddenly sped forward, then screeched to a halt. The driver flung the door open, and moving like a predator he snatched Jonathan off his bike, thrust him into the backseat and sped away.

Will and Nick, who were riding behind him, crashed into the fallen bike and dominoed onto the asphalt. Jesse screeched the van to a halt.

Lilah was already out of the car. "Leave the bikes!" she screamed. "Get into the house right now and call the police!"

She slammed her accelerator to the floor and went after Bruce.

Daniel had heard the noise and was already on the drive when Nick reached him, sobbing hysterically and flung his arms around Daniel's knees.

"Daniel," Will said shakily, "JJ's been kidnapped!"

"Don't wait for me," Jesse shouted from the street. "Call the police!"

DANIEL HAD NEVER BEEN so scared in his life. He hadn't been this scared when the Canadian guards had cuffed him and taken him into custody as a teen. Frustrated, but not scared.

"What kind of car was it?" He was running toward his truck.

"A station wagon like Maury's and Uncle Mike's," Will said, sprinting along beside him. "Lilah went after it."

Great. Thirty percent of the cars in Vermont were Subaru station wagons. "Go into the house and stay there with Jesse. I'll call the police from the truck," he said, and sped away.

He called the chief's direct line. "Bruce Jamison has kidnapped his son," he said succinctly. "My best guess is he's taking Route 30 over to I-91, and I'm seven, eight minutes behind him."

"I'll get a car out right now, then I'll alert the state police," the chief said. "You get any more information, call 9-1-1."

He should also have told the chief to look for Lilah and stop her from pursuing Bruce and her son. He'd deserted her, rejected her when she needed him most. How could he have been so selfish as to put himself, the boys, the center, first? Too wrapped up in his own feelings at having been lied to, he hadn't stopped to consider how much trouble *she* was in. Because he'd been so self-centered, now she was going to try to face down her ex-husband alone, and he knew she couldn't handle it. His panic escalated with every second that went by. He wasn't catching up to her, and he hadn't seen any gray station wagons.

In an agony of regret, Daniel drove like a maniac. He wasn't sure what he'd do if he came upon cows being herded across the road, blocking his path. The road out of the valley was rough, but it would be rough for Bruce, too, and he wasn't as familiar with the terrain as Daniel was.

He had a chance. There was hope. He chanted the thought to himself as he drove and drove and drove—toward what, he dreaded to find out.

THERE WAS NO HOPE. She couldn't catch Bruce's car. Sobs choked Lilah's throat and tears streamed down her face. For a few seconds she'd had the station wagon in her sights, and then it was gone, too far ahead to see.

This was all her fault. She should have gone to the pool, commanded Jonathan to get in the car and then fled the valley with nothing, not even the near-nothing with which they'd left Whittaker. She knew how cruel and resourceful Bruce was. She should have been ready for anything.

Now he had the most precious person in her life. Jonathan, probably scared to death, was under his control. She wouldn't give up until the last shred of hope vanished, but the road had twisted and turned, smaller roads had forked off in this direction and that. She had no idea if she was actually following Bruce anymore, but the one thing she couldn't do was go back to the apartment above the carriage house where she'd once been so happy to sit and wait. She'd go crazy.

In the distance, she heard the wail of a siren. She told herself the police were on their way to rescue Jonathan, and felt a second's relief until she realized the sound wasn't behind her, but off to one side. They were aiming for the freeway, and Bruce had gone in a different direction.

She had to call the police and tell them.

She braked and pulled over to the side, and just as she opened her phone, it rang. It could be Daniel, saying Jonathan was home safe and sound. Shaking with nerves and exhaustion, she answered the call.

"Mom?"

She had to calm down for his sake. "Jonathan. Are you all right?"

"I'm scared." He was crying. She felt as if she were bleeding inside.

"Lilah. Lilah, the good mother. Do you want your beloved son back?"

Bruce had taken the phone. He actually sounded amused. She leaned her head on the steering wheel and willed her voice to level out before she said another word. "What have you done to him?"

"Absolutely nothing except pick him up from the pool, just as any dad would. He's fine." Airline-pilot drawl. "But he sure misses his mommy. He's hoping you'll join us, so we can be the happy family we used to be."

"Where?" she said. It wasn't the moment to lash out at him. All that mattered was getting Jonathan back.

"We're up in that place where you took your boyfriend this afternoon." He delivered a stagy sigh. "I wish I'd thought to bring a camera to that meeting. The look on your face… Anyway, I followed the two of you when you took off, of course. And the rest is history. Oh, Lilah, poor woman, you've always underestimated me. I know how to get what I want."

"What *do* you want?" She bit her hand, just to keep from screaming.

"Like I said, meet us here, and the three of us will go away together. We'll go to another state, start all over. You are *such* a good bookkeeper, considering that you've only had one course in bookkeeping, but this time, Lilah," and now he dropped the fake country tone, let his innate cruelty show, "you *will* work with me, because you know what I'll do to you if you don't. And to Jonathan. By the way, come alone. No police, no boyfriend, just you. If I hear sirens, we're out of here."

If Bruce had called a second later, she would already have called the police and the cruisers would even now be exiting the freeway, heading in his direction with sirens screaming.

She felt faint. "I'll come alone. If Jonathan isn't all right when I get there, I'll kill you, Bruce, with my bare hands."

"As if." He chuckled, and hung up.

He'd always underestimated her, too, but he didn't know it. That was her trump card. Hands shaking, she dialed Daniel's cell. The voice that answered sounded as panicked as hers. She spoke rapidly. "Bruce has taken Jonathan to our hideout in the woods. Call the police and tell them they're on the wrong track, just to go back to the station and call off the search, because Bruce said I had to come alone."

She slammed the phone shut, turned the car around and drove as if a pride of lions was chasing her.

DANIEL SWORE AS HE HADN'T sworn in years. He'd almost reached the freeway, far from where Bruce held Jonathan captive.

He made a screeching U-turn, then called the police dispatcher. He wouldn't call them off, he'd tell them where to go. "Here's where they are," he said, and tersely gave directions, "and *no sirens!*"

LILAH LEFT THE CAR BLOCKING the bottom of the logging road and hid the keys in the crook of a small tree. Bruce would find it difficult to escape with Jonathan. Halfway up the hill, she made a megaphone of her hands and called out, "Jonathan, everything's going to be okay. I'm here."

"Come on down," Bruce said, doing a passable impression of a game show host. "Or up in this case."

She entered the clearing. It was darker in the woods than it had been on the road, but she could see Bruce standing beside his car and holding Jonathan in front of him. Not holding him so much as containing him. Jonathan wriggled, trying to run to her, but Bruce got an even tighter grip on him.

Jonathan was crying, holding out his arms to Lilah. She couldn't stand it. She rushed toward him fiercely. She'd rip him away from Bruce, run down the road with him, get him into the car—and Bruce would catch up with them in about fifteen seconds, probably before she'd even started the engine.

No, she had to ignore Jonathan's distress, startle Bruce with her calm, collected behavior, take the upper hand. "Don't worry, baby," she said soothingly. "Dad and I are going to talk. We'll work things out." She smiled at Bruce, enjoying the surprise on his face.

How had she dredged up that even smile? No time to think about it now, just keep using it on Bruce.

Several feet away from them, she said, "Okay, Bruce, I give up. You're right. We should all be together again."

The startled look Jonathan sent her broke her heart. *Trust me. Go along with me.* She said the words over and over in her mind as she went toward him, hoping he'd somehow receive the message.

Miraculously, he calmed down. Maybe he knew, or maybe he just felt better the closer she came to him.

"You are so smart!" she said to Bruce. "How did you get my cell number?"

"It was no trouble at all. Jonathan was happy to call you for me." His tone was teasing.

"And I was happy to hear from him," Lilah said smoothly. "So, here we are. Tell me again, Bruce, what do you have in mind for us?" She'd stall him until she could make a plan of action, because whatever she came up with had to work. She'd only have one chance.

He tilted his head toward the sky. "I've always liked the idea of settling into one of those midwestern states. You know, good schools, polite people. People with a certain…innocence."

"Oh," she breathed, "I see where you're going. Do you already have a new money-making scheme?"

"Yes." He looked smug. "But you don't think I'm stupid enough to tell you about it yet, do you?"

"Heavens, no. But I know it will be a good one." She gave him a thoughtful look, moving another step closer. "What will we live on while you're just starting up?"

"I managed to stash away quite a bit of money before you—" He halted. "But that's in the past, isn't it?" he said genially. "We're moving forward now."

She was, at least, inch by inch. "Bruce, if we do resume our former lives, we have to agree on a couple of issues. You have to treat me nicely. You can't use verbal or physical abuse. No secrets this time, either. We work together as a team."

Bruce's eyes narrowed. "We'll be like Bonnie and Clyde," he said. "I'll do the scamming and you'll fix the books. We'll look like everybody else in Podunk until somebody uncovers us, and then we'll move and start all over again. Jonathan will be a well-traveled young man, won't you, son?"

Lilah felt sick. But she had to maintain the act. Bruce seemed to be buying it. "It sounds as if you've thought it out well." She took one more small step. "So let's start by being friends again. We can work out everything else later."

He let go of Jonathan, which was all she'd hoped for, and he ran straight into her arms.

DANIEL'S HEART WAS THUDDING when he reached the bottom of the logging road and found Lilah's car blocking it. He parked the truck and started up the hill.

He wanted to run, but he knew he had to move slowly and silently.

At last he heard voices, two voices at least, and it gave him hope that at the end of his quest he'd find all three of them, Lilah, Bruce and Jonathan. When he was as close to the clearing as he could get without making his presence known, he saw the scene ahead of him.

Jonathan was behind Lilah, clutching her waist. She stood close to Bruce. She was smiling. Bruce seemed to be taken by that smile. *What was going on here?*

Daniel wanted to throw himself into the space remaining between the two of them, somehow get both Lilah and Jonathan behind him and destroy the man, but something held him back. Could she actually be making a deal with Bruce, or was she conning him in the way he'd conned so many innocent people?

He wouldn't blame her for making a deal to save her son. He supposed he'd do almost anything to save one of his brothers, one of his boys—or Lilah and Jonathan.

He crept closer, ready for anything.

"So you agree to my conditions? You get your temper under control, we cooperate with each other, and above all, we do the best thing for Jonathan."

"Whatever works for you, baby, works for me."

She was conning him! His head spinning, Daniel crouched down, ready to leap forward when he needed to. He couldn't count on the police to arrive in time. When he moved, he'd have to move fast.

LILAH'S ONLY CONNECTION to reality was the tug of Jonathan's hands on her waist, the stifled sounds of his sobs. Except for that, she was in another sphere, where the real Lilah had ceased to exist and a stranger had taken her place. Confidently, she took yet another step toward Bruce.

*I'm almost there.* She had a plan in place now. "When I said we'd start by being friends," she said, batting her eyelashes, "you know I didn't mean *just* friends."

Surely she'd gone too far. He sounded wary for the first time. "Hey," he said, "what's made you so friendly all of a sudden?"

She sighed, held out her hands in a defeated gesture. "Well, Bruce, I've had to admit you're smarter than I am. You've won. I want Jonathan to have a happy life, so I might as well try to make it work with you, turn this back into a happy marriage. You are his father. I'm sure that with a lot of attention and affection he'll grow to admire you as much as I have. Besides," she said, daring a smile again, "I've tried being poor, and I found out it was a lot more fun to be rich. And you know how to make us rich better than anybody I know."

He seemed mollified. "I can sure do that."

*Now. Do it now.* Fighting down her disgust, she took that last crucial step. "And I know that once we're working together toward a common goal, we'll become closer, in every way—"

A glance at his leering smile was all she needed. When he held out his arms to her, she gathered up all her strength and drove her knee hard into his groin.

He yelled in pain and fell to the ground. She delivered a solid kick to his shin and then, for good measure, another one to his shoulder.

Footsteps thundered close behind her, but there was no fear left in her anymore. She had only had one person to fear, and he was down for the count. She'd won the match.

DANIEL LIFTED JONATHAN off his feet and wrapped his arms around both of them. "Oh, Lilah, Lilah," was all he was able to say. Her adrenaline sapped, she was shaking like an aspen tree in fall. He held her upright. On her own, she would have collapsed. She buried her face in his chest, and he held them both, whispering comfort, delivering love.

"I've been so unfair to you," he choked out. "I'm not the person I seem to be, either. Mike and Ian aren't my brothers in the way you think. I'll tell you everything later. Now all I want to do is tell you how much I…"

"Daniel," Jonathan interrupted him. "Mom did it. She saved us. All by herself! With the soccer moves we taught her."

His eyes were so wide, shining in the gathering dusk, and his pride so evident, that Daniel had to smile down at him. "She sure did. She's wonderful, isn't she?" Lilah made a slight movement against his chest.

"Awesome," Jonathan breathed. "You are, too," he said kindly. "But I was sort of thinking if you married her, she could take care of both of us."

Lilah's head shot upward. "Jonathan!"

Daniel snuggled her back against him. "I've never had a finer proposal, Jonathan, and I accept. Lilah, is there any reason we three should not be joined in holy…"

Her soft laughter echoed in his heart. She gazed up

at him. "No matter what's happened in your past, no, absolutely none."

Jonathan's arms tightened around Daniel's neck, Lilah's around his chest and his heart beat with a love so strong that it overwhelmed him. Inches away, the chief of police and one of Churchill's two deputies were handcuffing a groaning Bruce and reading him his rights, but the scene couldn't get inside his head.

Only one thing mattered to him now. At long last, Daniel had a real family.

# *Epilogue*

*Three weeks later...*

"How do I look?"

Lilah smiled. How Jonathan looked was very grown up in his navy suit, white shirt and blue striped tie.

"Movie-star handsome," she told him, bursting with pride in her son.

"I feel kinda dumb," he said, fiddling with his tie.

Lilah pointed out the back door. "You're dressed exactly like the other boys."

And like Daniel. She caught a glimpse of him and wanted nothing more than to rush into his arms. She loved him, she loved Mike and Ian, the boys, Jesse. She'd be marrying all of them—gladly.

She gazed affectionately at the boys as they escorted guests to the folding chairs that filled the backyard, each of them so prim and proper as he held out an arm for a female guest. The yard was green, manicured and lovely. The arbor where she and Daniel would take their vows was surrounded by vases of white lilies mixed with dark-blue flax. A thrill went through her. She'd be standing before that arbor soon, saying, "I do," and thinking, *Oh, yes, I do*.

Quite a crowd had come to see him get married. Rightfully so. He was the most wonderful man she'd ever known.

"You know, Jonathan, I have you to thank for this."

"Because I proposed?" he said. "Well, somebody had to."

She laughed. "That, too," she said. "If you hadn't wanted to spend the night with Nick so badly, we'd have gone back to the forest and we would never have seen them again."

"Hey," he said, "I did do it, didn't I?"

Dana, who would be Lilah's only attendant, rushed into the room, resplendent in a long, lovely blue-flowered dress that complemented Lilah's pale-blue organdy one. She put her arms around Lilah. "I'm so happy for you," she said. "I'm even happier for Daniel." She stood back and looked at Lilah. "When you ran away," she said softly, "I'm so glad you ran away to us."

So was Lilah. Two months ago, who would have thought her life would turn out so wonderfully? Bruce was now just a memory. He'd been arrested, charged not only with kidnapping Jonathan but also with frauds he'd committed before he moved to Whittaker that had just now come to light. This time he was facing many years in prison, and, to Lilah's relief, he had lost his parental rights to Jonathan. When she and Daniel got back from their honeymoon at a romantic seaside resort in Maine, Daniel would start the process of adopting Jonathan. Her heart swelled with love. They'd be a real family.

Mike stepped through the kitchen door, interrupting her thoughts. She'd gotten closer to Daniel's brothers since they'd realized how much she and Daniel meant to each other.

"It'll be good to have a woman in the family," he said, giving her a bear hug. "Keep him in line, okay? Ian and I are sick and tired of doing it all by ourselves."

"He is a wild one," she said, laughing as she hugged him back.

"Am I interrupting anything?"

It was Ian, and she still wasn't sure what to expect from him. She was touched when he patted her arm and said, "Make him happy."

"I'll do my very best," she said. Better than best.

"Daniel's fit to be tied," Jesse said, banging the door behind him. "Are we about ready in here?"

DANIEL FIDGETED AS HE TRIED to concentrate on greeting each guest in a personal way. He could only think about Lilah. In just a few minutes, she'd be his, and he intended to make her the happiest woman in the universe. In a couple of months, Jonathan would be his, too. He loved Lilah's son. He hoped they'd have a dozen more just like him, maybe with a girl thrown in somewhere.

He gazed at each of his boys, one at a time. Maury, happy beyond belief to be working for Mike at the diner. He'd already found his dream.

Will, who'd soon be back at home with his parents.

Nick. Would he ever solve the mystery of Nick? The boy was happier every day and no longer had nightmares, but he still kept his secret locked tightly inside him.

Then Daniel's gaze drifted toward Jason, who was standing straight and tall at the back of the rows of chairs, his eyes on Melissa, whom he'd just seated. He might ask Lilah how she'd feel about having one more child right now, a big one, already toilet-trained. He smiled. He knew what her answer would be.

But where in the heck was she? If she'd backed out, he'd...

"She's ready," Jesse said at his elbow. "Everybody and his next-of-kin wanted to congratulate her. The kitchen's plumb full."

The music swelled, filling the air with a melody as close to "The Wedding March" as the high school's chamber music quartet could reach. Ian and Mike stepped out the kitchen door and stood beside him at the arbor, where Reverend Galloway, looking properly solemn, stood waiting.

"Keep it short," he whispered, and Galloway gave him a reproving look.

Dana came down the aisle and stood on the other side of the arbor. Now Daniel could only gaze longingly toward the kitchen door, waiting for the glorious moment when—

His heart lurched. There she was, so beautiful in her pale-blue organdy dress she made his heart skip a beat. Jonathan stood by her side, his arm through hers, looking happy to be giving his mother away. As she came down the aisle, their gazes met and held.

And kept on holding as they said their vows, and as he shared his love for her in his kiss and accepted hers with joy. It wasn't easy to end that kiss, but when he did, he smiled down at her.

"Have I told you today that I love you?"

"One or two…" She paused. "Or maybe thirty times. But don't stop now. I'll never get tired of hearing it."

"So I can say it again?"

"Oh, yes," she said, "but I'll go first. I love you, Daniel, with my whole heart, and I always will."

There were tears in her eyes. He put his arm around her as they walked up the aisle to cheers and clapping, then bent his head to whisper in her ear. "My turn. I love you, Lilah Foster," he said. "I love you, I love you, I love you, I…"

What miracle had sent her into his life? What miracle had sent him here to wait for her to come into his life? At long last, they'd both found the place where they belonged—beside each other.

*Celebrate Harlequin's 60th anniversary with*
*Harlequin® Superromance®*
*and the DIAMOND LEGACY miniseries!*

*Follow the stories of four cousins as they come to*
*terms with the complications of love and what it means*
*to be a family. Discover with them the sixty-year-old*
*secret that rocks not one but two families in...*
*A DAUGHTER'S TRUST by Tara Taylor Quinn.*

*Available in September 2009 from*
*Harlequin® Superromance®*

RICK'S APPOINTMENT with his attorney early Wednesday morning went only moderately better than his meeting with social services the day before. The prognosis wasn't great—but at least his attorney was going to file a motion for DNA testing. Just so Rick could petition to see the child...his sister's baby. The sister he didn't know he had until it was too late.

The rest of what his attorney said had been downhill from there.

Cell phone in hand before he'd even reached his Nitro, Rick punched in the speed dial number he'd programmed the day before.

Maybe foster parent Sue Bookman hadn't received his message. Or had lost his number. Maybe she didn't want to talk to him. At this point he didn't much care what she wanted.

"Hello?" She answered before the first ring was complete. And sounded breathless.

Young and breathless.

"Ms. Bookman?"

"Yes. This is Rick Kraynick, right?"

"Yes, ma'am."

"I recognized your number on caller ID," she said, her voice uneven, as though she was still engaged in whatever physical activity had her so breathless to begin with. "I'm sorry I didn't get back to you. I've been a little...distracted."

The words came in more disjointed spurts. Was she jogging?

"No problem," he said, when, in fact, he'd spent the better part of the night before watching his phone. And fretting. "Did I get you at a bad time?"

"No worse than usual," she said, adding, "Better than some. So, how can I help?"

God, if only this could be so easy. He'd ask. She'd help. And life could go well. At least for one little person in his family.

It would be a first.

"Mr. Kraynick?"

"Yes. Sorry. I was...are you sure there isn't a better time to call?"

"I'm bouncing a baby, Mr. Kraynick. It's what I do."

"Is it Carrie?" he asked quickly, his pulse racing.

"How do you know Carrie?" She sounded defensive, which wouldn't do him any good.

"I'm her uncle," he explained, "her mother's— Christy's—older brother, and I know you have her."

"I can neither confirm nor deny your allegations, Mr. Kraynick. Please call social services." She rattled off the number.

"Wait!" he said, unable to hide his urgency. "Please," he said more calmly. "Just hear me out."

"How did you find me?"

"A friend of Christy's."

"I'm sorry I can't help you, Mr. Kraynick," she said softly. "This conversation is over."

"I grew up in foster care," he said, as though that gave him some special privilege. Some insider's edge.

"Then you know you shouldn't be calling me at all."

"Yes… But Carrie is my niece," he said. "I need to see her. To know that she's okay."

"You'll have to go through social services to arrange that."

"I'm sure you know it's not as easy as it sounds. I'm a single man with no real ties and I've no intention of petitioning for custody. They aren't real eager to give me the time of day. I never even knew Carrie's mother. For all intents and purposes, our mother didn't raise either one of us. All I have going for me is half a set of genes. My lawyer's on it, but it could be weeks— months—before this is sorted out. Carrie could be adopted by then. Which would be fine, great for her, but then I'd have lost my chance. I don't want to take her. I won't hurt her. I just have to see her."

"I'm sorry, Mr. Kraynick, but…"

\* \* \* \* \*

*Find out if Rick Kraynick will ever have a chance to meet his niece.*
*Look for A DAUGHTER'S TRUST*
*by Tara Taylor Quinn,*
*available in September 2009.*

We'll be spotlighting a different series
every month throughout 2009
to celebrate our 60th anniversary.

**Look for Harlequin® Superromance®
in September!**

*Celebrate with
The Diamond Legacy
miniseries!*

Follow the stories of four cousins as they come to terms
with the complications of love and what it means to
be a family. Discover with them the sixty-year-old secret
that rocks not one but two families.

A DAUGHTER'S TRUST by *Tara Taylor Quinn*
**September**

FOR THE LOVE OF FAMILY by *Kathleen O'Brien*
**October**

LIKE FATHER, LIKE SON by *Karina Bliss*
**November**

A MOTHER'S SECRET by *Janice Kay Johnson*
**December**

**Available wherever books are sold.**

# You're invited to join our Tell Harlequin Reader Panel!

By joining our new reader panel you will:

- Receive Harlequin® books—they are FREE and yours to keep with no obligation to purchase anything!
- Participate in fun online surveys
- Exchange opinions and ideas with women just like you
- Have a say in our new book ideas and help us publish the best in women's fiction

*In addition, you will have a chance to win great prizes and receive special gifts! See Web site for details. Some conditions apply. Space is limited.*

To join, visit us at

## www.TellHarlequin.com.

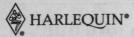

# The Ranger's Secret
## REBECCA WINTERS

When Yosemite Park ranger Chase Jarvis rescues
an injured passenger from a downed helicopter,
he is stunned to discover it's the woman he
once loved. But Chase is no longer the man
Annie Bower knew. Will she forgive him for
the secret he's been keeping for ten long years?
And will he forgive Annie for her own secret—
the daughter Chase didn't know he had...?

*Available September
wherever books are sold.*

In 2009 Harlequin celebrates
60 years of pure reading pleasure!

We're marking this occasion by offering
16 **FREE** full books to download and read.

Visit

# www.HarlequinCelebrates.com

to choose from a variety of
great romance stories
that are absolutely **FREE!**

(Total approximate retail value of $60)

We invite you to visit and share the Web site
with your friends, family
and anyone who enjoys reading.

# REQUEST YOUR FREE BOOKS!
## 2 FREE NOVELS PLUS 2
# FREE GIFTS!

*American ★ Romance*®

## Love, Home & Happiness!

**YES!** Please send me 2 FREE Harlequin® American Romance® novels and my 2 FREE gifts (gifts are worth about $10). After receiving them, if I don't wish to receive any more books, I can return the shipping statement marked "cancel." If I don't cancel, I will receive 4 brand-new novels every month and be billed just $4.24 per book in the U.S. or $4.99 per book in Canada.* That's a savings of close to 15% off the cover price! It's quite a bargain! Shipping and handling is just 50¢ per book. I understand that accepting the 2 free books and gifts places me under no obligation to buy anything. I can always return a shipment and cancel at any time. Even if I never buy another book from Harlequin, the two free books and gifts are mine to keep forever.

154 HDN EYSE   354 HDN EYSQ

Name _____ (PLEASE PRINT) _____

Address _____ Apt. # _____

City _____ State/Prov. _____ Zip/Postal Code _____

Signature (if under 18, a parent or guardian must sign)

### Mail to the **Harlequin Reader Service:**
**IN U.S.A.:** P.O. Box 1867, Buffalo, NY 14240-1867
**IN CANADA:** P.O. Box 609, Fort Erie, Ontario L2A 5X3

Not valid to current subscribers of Harlequin® American Romance® books.

**Want to try two free books from another line?**
**Call 1-800-873-8635 or visit www.morefreebooks.com.**

\* Terms and prices subject to change without notice. Prices do not include applicable taxes. N.Y. residents add applicable sales tax. Canadian residents will be charged applicable provincial taxes and GST. Offer not valid in Quebec. This offer is limited to one order per household. All orders subject to approval. Credit or debit balances in a customer's account(s) may be offset by any other outstanding balance owed by or to the customer. Please allow 4 to 6 weeks for delivery. Offer available while quantities last.

**Your Privacy:** Harlequin is committed to protecting your privacy. Our Privacy Policy is available online at www.eHarlequin.com or upon request from the Reader Service. From time to time we make our lists of customers available to reputable third parties who may have a product or service of interest to you. If you would prefer we not share your name and address, please check here. ☐

HAR09R

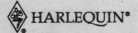

**HARLEQUIN®**

*American ★ Romance*®

# COMING NEXT MONTH
## Available September 8, 2009

**#1273 DOCTOR DADDY by Jacqueline Diamond**
*Men Made in America*
Dr. Jane McKay wants a child more than anything, but her dreams
of parenthood don't include the sexy, maddening doctor next door.
Luke Van Dam is *not* ready to settle down. Yet the gorgeous babe magnet
seems to attract *babies,* too—he's just become guardian of an infant girl.
Is Luke the right man to share Jane's dream after all?

**#1274 ONCE A COP by Lisa Childs**
*Citizen's Police Academy*
Roberta "Robbie" Meyers wants a promotion out of the Lakewood P.D. vice
squad so she can spend more time with her daughter. Holden Thomas sees only a
woman with a job that's too dangerous for a mother. So the bachelor guardian
strikes Robbie off his list of mommy candidates for the little girl under his care.
Too bad he can't resist the attractive cop's charms!

**#1275 THE RANGER'S SECRET by Rebecca Winters**
When Chase Jarvis rescues an injured passenger from a downed helicopter, the
Yosemite ranger is stunned to discover it's the woman he once loved. But he is
no longer the man Annie Bower knew. Will she forgive him for the secret he's
been keeping for ten long years? And will he forgive Annie her own secret—the
daughter Chase didn't know he had…?

**#1276 A WEDDING FOR BABY by Laura Marie Altom**
*Baby Boom*
Gabby Craig's pregnancy is a dream come true. Too bad the father is an
unreliable, no-good charmer who's left town. And when his brother, Dane, steps
in to help, Gabby can't help relying on the handsome, *responsible* judge. But
how can she be falling for the brother of her baby's daddy?

www.eHarlequin.com

HARCNMBPA0809